LIFE IN YOUR WORLD

ANJ CAIRNS

Copyright © Anj Cairns 2017

The author has asserted their moral right under the Copyright, Designs and Patents Act 1988 to be identified as the author of this work.

All rights reserved. No part of this publication may be reproduced, copied, stored in a retrieval system or transmitted, in any form or by any means, without the prior written consent of the copyright holder, nor be otherwise circulated in any form of binding or cover than that in which it is published and without a similar condition being imposed on the subsequent purchaser.

Disclaimer

This is a work of fiction. Names, characters, places and incidents are either the products of the author's imagination or are used fictitiously, and any resemblance to actual persons, living or dead is entirely coincidental. Certain businesses and organisations are mentioned, but the stories playing out in them are wholly imaginary.

For my dad, whose energy stays with me always.

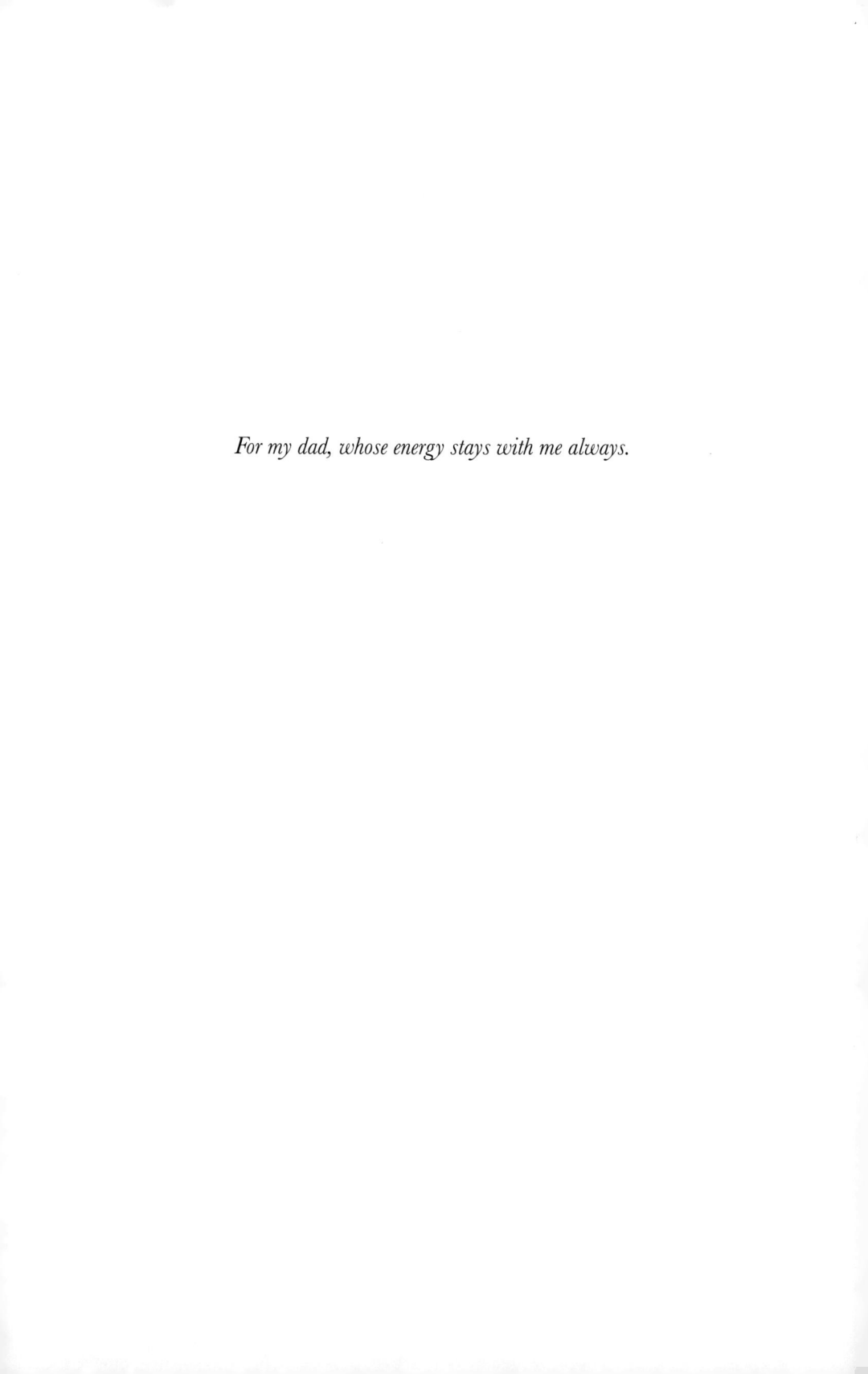

The Core

Chapter 1

A MONSTROUS PULSE vibrated through the Core. Its sound waves shook the interior and roused its many inhabitants from their state of stillness.

"SKETCH!"

Fearful she had used her last chance, Sketch crept from her allocated space. The surrounding atmosphere darkened as she picked her way towards the furious voice. Her essence convulsed, causing her to stumble. The unlit pathway contracted as she progressed towards its pitch-black terminal. The two entities faced each other.

"What is your role?" said the One, in low tone vibrations inaudible to the rest of the Core's inhabitants.

Sketch quivered.

"It's…"

"'It's' is not a sufficient answer. There is a delay in your response," said the One. "You have shown me you do not comprehend the gravity of your errors or their consequences for those we serve."

Sketch's aura dipped. She scanned the available data for an appropriate response.

"You are supposed to be waiting, to be vigilant. And most of all you are required to be responsive."

"I attempted to react but—"

"Do not interrupt. If you can't even answer my questions how will we ever be able to trust you with the most basic of duties?"

"I'm still new. I never meant to upset anyone. It's not my fault the boy was upset. I like the boy," said Sketch.

The space between them remained unlit, but Sketch detected a fractional reduction of tension. She shifted. The silence was more unpleasant than the darkness.

"You are inexperienced. This is accurate."

A spark of light emitted from Sketch's being and hung in the atmosphere before fizzling to nothing.

"I'm going to give you a choice," said the One. "You can opt to leave the Core, take the offer of a transformation and begin anew."

Sketch trembled.

"Alternatively, you will undergo further training to acquire the dexterity necessary to continue in your current position. Errors will be scrutinized; you will be observed and should you fail, the consequences will be severe. Consider the options."

"Consideration is not required. I select the training."

"So it will be entered into the data," said the One.

There were no further pulses, and after a prolonged pause Sketch considered the encounter concluded. Her light levels returned to normal. She hadn't chosen this existence but wished to stay. She was in awe of those vibrant, stimulating energies who perfected each transaction at the first attempt, an ability that continued to elude her.

Sketch searched for Inco and isolated him within the swarm of vibrations and temperatures at work in the Core. She moved within his proximity.

"I have been reassigned to work with Virder for extra training. My existence is tentative but still in place," she said.

"That's amazing. I thought you'd be sent for transformation given the high level of errors you've logged," he said. Inco lit up, matching the vibrancy of her aura.

"So did I. It was an option."

"It is known that the One is just in adjudications."

"Just but terrifying," said Sketch.

"So, what shall we do until our shift time begins?" he asked. "Now you are no longer at risk."

"I desire to go and watch the humans. Can we go and observe the boy? I like him," said Sketch eagerly. "And I want to make sure he's alright after what happened earlier."

Inco lost light from his aura. "Perhaps it's preferable to leave him alone. He may still be angry."

"Do you think?" asked Sketch.

"Would you not prefer to be stationary for a time. Prepare for tomorrow's training? I cannot understand your attraction to a human."

"Please," she said, changing her energy signature to a pleading light grey. "Just for one half hour time unit."

"Okay, we will do as you suggest."

She spiraled patterns of light as Inco gave in to her request.

Sketch and Inco observed the human boy, who showed no signs of knowing he was being watched. He sat in front of the family desktop computer, a clip-on webcam perched on top of its cumbersome monitor. The machine was too old to have a built-in camera and microphone. Matt attempted to connect to Skype, with the aid of an old-fashioned headset. It came with foam headphone covers and a microphone that stuck out in front of him on a piece of metal attached to the plastic arc crammed on top of his unruly hair.

"This is embarrassing," he said. "Who am I kidding? Even if I can make this ancient pile of crap work, I can't call Britney looking like this."

He removed the headset, shoving it into the back of the wooden bureau doubling as a desk, exited Skype and opened the web browser to the site where he published his blog and began to type.

Inco pulsated darkness.

"I don't understand why you're fixated on the human boy. He is negative, unfriendly, has unrealistic expectations about everything and doesn't like anyone," he said.

"Not everyone. He likes the one called Britney," Sketch said. "Oh, observe. He's updating on the Internet." She focused on the keystrokes as they formed into human text.

My mum really doesn't like anything new. She won't upgrade our computer to something from this century, get me a laptop for school or even an iPad. Any of those things would help me to look normal, not be seen as some weirdo poor kid.

She's got a good job but she's such a freaking hippie, hates buying new things, and she spends hours shopping in those second-hand shops where all the clothes stink of the old and dead. I've tried to make her see how you need to stay up-to-date to be accepted, but she's determined to stick with this ancient reconditioned PC until its components disintegrate. I swear that day better be coming soon.

If it weren't for my dad, I'd still be listening to music on an ancient CD Walkman. At least I can take the iPod he bought me to school without shame. Now all I have to do is make this stupid computer sync with the iPod. You'd think that would be simple enough, but it's like there's some evil computer god who's got it in for me.

Matt paused his two-fingered typing, took out his iPod and began to untangle the cables from their knotted ball to connect to the computer.

"Oh Inco, he's making that screwed up face again. Look at how his nose gets all crinkled. Look Inco. Isn't he the most human human you've ever observed?" Sketch fizzled as she took in each moment of the boy fiddling with the cables. She bubbled and crackled, giving out an aura of near maximum light. "I am vibrant, so vibrant," she said.

"It's not like you've seen many humans, though, is it?" said Inco, his darkness a sharp contrast with her luminosity.

"No," said Sketch, her sparkling aura dulling. "But I've seen some. There's this gorgeous boy, his female, the pack leader who birthed him and… Well, I'm sure I've seen more than that but I can't remember their names."

Inco turned from Sketch and the boy.

"I'm going," he said. "You should, too. There is little else to observe."

"But there might be, and I must practise anticipating the unexpected so I will observe for a while more."

Sketch's obsession with Matt didn't help her progress towards the qualification she required. She commenced each block with determination, ready to put what she had learnt into practice, but thoughts of the boy would fight their way passed her resolve until she found herself disconnecting from the stream at inconvenient moments. Distractions such as this were what put her at risk of transformation and an unknown future existence.

She turned her attention back to Matt as he turned off the computer, calling it all kinds of unfavourable names during the five minutes it took to power down. He trudged up the stairs with a packet of bourbon biscuits balanced on top of a steaming cup of builders' tea.

"Night, boy Matt," said Sketch.

As the time approached for Sketch to begin her session with Virder, she skittered from position to position around the Core, unable to focus on any particular piece of data or process. Despite her nervousness, she was determined the actions she performed during the slot would be precise, free from error and delivered without delay. The thought of undergoing a transformation did not sit comfortably with any of the energies in the Core, but for Sketch the possibility represented more than a fleeting nightmare. If she didn't show improvement, it would happen to her.

"Welcome, young Sketch." Virder gravitated across the busy workspace toward her.

"Hello."

"You're giving off darkness. Are you afraid? There is no need for fear. It's all a matter of logic. Dead easy, as the humans say. There will be someone with you at all times, so fill with light and we will begin," he communicated. Sketch's aura took on the appearance of pale, winter morning sunlight.

"What shall I do?"

"First off, I would like you to simply absorb. Stay with me, take in what I do and then, if you feel brave enough, I'll hand over to you."

"Okay," said Sketch, lightening further.

"I like to have faith in Starters. They keep you dormant for far too long. The best way to learn is to do the job. This is how learning takes place, during sessions with physical humans and their irregular behaviours."

After many periods of service, Virder remained unparalleled amongst inhabitants of the Core. His pulse had a gravity akin to that of a human god. He could answer more questions than anyone, aside from the One. All the Starters were allotted sessions to absorb him as part as their sublimation into the Core. This resulted in many energies becoming overly attracted to him, despite his elevated position and standing.

He stationed himself in the readiness and indicated Sketch should join him.

"You will find the waiting challenging, frustrating, boring even. But it's the waiting that is important. If you become distracted for even a short period, you may miss the signal. And in such cases, it can be problematic to regain tempo, so be vigilant."

Sketch stilled herself, leveling her light and the buzz that it created. Her mentor had put her anxieties to rest, for the moment.

It became apparent, as her mentor had indicated, that significant time could pass before any sign of activity emerged, so Sketch took the opportunity to quiz Virder.

"The human boy, the one named Matt, he doesn't know many girl humans, does he?" asked Sketch.

"Let's see," said Virder. "He's got four hundred and fifty-seven friends on Facebook and a similar number on Snapchat and Instagram. A fair few of them are boy humans – the majority it seems."

"Does he not like girls?"

"Oh, he likes them. He spends most of his time online just gazing at their profiles."

Sketch's aura dimmed.

"The one called Britney, he likes her more than the rest. He's always hovering over her profile. Never writes on her timeline. Sometimes thinks about it," said Virder.

"What's she like? The Britney one."

"She's his age, got white hair that's extra straight. She makes it so by applying dangerously hot metal to the strands emerging from her head. This is human hair fashion. Everything is always the same on her face. She colours it with the orange liquid they call foundation and then adds black mascara, eyeliner and metallic gold powder on her eyes. In human language, she has pouty lips filled with pink stick colour to make them appear larger."

She considered his words, struggling with the idea of colours that didn't exist in the Core.

"Why does he not send her a message?" asked Sketch. "Why does he ignore her if he likes her so much?"

"There's much you've got to learn about the humans. They have much strangeness in them."

"What do you mean by strangeness?"

"They can be contradictory, wanting one thing and doing another. In this case, it stems from his shyness," said Virder.

"What is shyness?"

"Think about Starters. Some of you radiate light from the beginning and others need a little more coaxing to build their way from darkness."

"So the boy feels dark and needs help to become light?"

"In the case of his relations with the girl human Britney, this would be correct."

Sketch let the idea of shyness flow through her and found she understood it. By applying Virder's description, she categorized herself as shy, too. With the qualifieds in the Core in particular.

A loud buzzing noise surrounded them, indicating an error had occurred.

"That'll be problems in sector 10d – it's always in 10d," said Virder. "It'll need to be addressed before it begins to affect the humans." He withdrew from his stationary position. Sketch rose to follow him.

"Sorry, Starter. Someone needs to remain stationed here. You'll be error free."

Sketch observed his pulsating aura gravitated way from her position.

"I'll be error free?"

She darted backwards and forwards, running through his guidance.

"Wait for the signal. Don't disrupt the tempo. Learn about the humans. Learn about the humans."

She lit up. The boy was a human. Ergo, she should spend her time waiting to learn about him. With the knowledge she would acquire, she was less likely to disrupt the tempo when the session commenced. Sketch set about accessing his social media accounts. She noted he had two thousand and thirty-four photos posted on the Internet. Posting pictures must be an important activity for humans, she mused. Many of the images she located through her search, showed the boy's friends and family and, although she didn't understand why, she was pleased to find most of them contained few female humans.

As she rummaged through his online footprint, posts, comments and status updates appeared from his friends and groups he followed. One human stood out from the others: Ashling Peterson. She noticed the female often tried to interact with him, commenting on and liking his content. The photo she used on all her networks appeared odd to Sketch. It was of a newborn human infant. Could miniature humans communicate via words at such an early stage in their growth? After a further probing, she discovered a series of images showing a fatigued-but-smiling Ashling holding the baby featured in the pictures. Sketch surmised the infant must be her offspring. If so, it would follow she was also kind. Humans with children are known to be compassionate so they can look after them. Ashling's face was softer in the photos with the baby. Despite the female's repeated attempts to communicate with Matt, he ignored her comments.

Why would the girl continue? queried Sketch, unable to make sense of the data.

A high tone vibration reverberated and Sketch became alert. There he was. The boy. The distance between the two of them disappeared.

"Oh," said Sketch. "I could almost reach out from the Core, into his world, and explore his face." She'd never been so close to a human before. Her functions began to stall as a combination of excitement and nerves began to surge through her being. She shook herself but failed to regain control.

It is not a positive time for me to freeze, she thought. *I can't make him wait, not under any circumstances.*

Sketch tried again to react in a manner appropriate to her role, to reactivate her critical functions, but her increased attempts only resulted in more panic.

"Ancient pile of shit!" he said, swigging back a gulp of his morning can of Coke.

The reactions of the boy escalated Sketch's level of anxiety. She had no comprehension of what to do in this situation. She was in 10a, after all. She shouldn't have been left alone. Why had they left her alone? Now everyone would be able to see what a mess she was making. They'd all know what a failure she was. Her aura spun and spiralled, spitting out violent sparks unpleasant to observe.

A buzzer screeched. Sketch spun around but failed to locate any assistance. With the energy shortages and Virder dealing with the event in 10d, Sketch was alone. She oscillated between light and darkness, unable to control her actions or thoughts. In a final attempt to rescue the situation, she summoned up all her energy and projected it.

"They will recycle me for certain now and I'll end up somewhere awful like—"

Her words were ensnared by the blackest darkness before everything turned a vibrant royal blue.

THE ONE OMITTED an absence of light. Reserves were low and conserving power was a priority in the aftermath of the earlier breakdown. What was Virder thinking leaving an unqualified in charge? And not just any Starter but the one who consistently failed to meet targets or make any progression to a higher level of functioning.

Sketch is my responsibility, the One thought. *I am the most senior. She is incompetent, unconfident and a poor fit with the vital actions of the Core. If I don't take appropriate action, worse will occur. It's my operational duty to recommend recycling.*

The One summoned a trembling Sketch into its zone having come to a decision.

"I'm sure you have plenty to say for yourself but I don't think your comments are relevant. It is clear you caused the shutdown through negligence. In doing so you have put our existence at risk."

Sketch focused downwards, her aura dimmed to its lowest light level.

"I've thought in depth about this and because you were left unsupervised, and only because of this, I've decided not to send you for recycling, yet."

A small, pale yellow glow radiated out from Sketch.

"There must be consequences for your actions. There are always consequences. You are not exempt from them. However, we've invested much into your training and the energy expended in doing so cannot go to waste. There is no place for such misuse in the Core."

Sketch quivered, struggling to maintain a positive flush.

"You will be sent to the human world for a period of six weeks, during which time you must learn their ways, understand their needs and how your mistakes affect their lives."

Many of the Core's inhabitants found the idea of departing its boundaries abhorrent. But the external realm contained humans, and for Sketch this meant the boy, Matt, who existed there in corporeal form. Sketch tried to suppress a sudden lightness. The temporary banishment was supposed to be a punishment for the earlier disastrous manoeuvrings.

"Before you transform, you'll receive a briefing about your assignment, your work placement, and crucial information about being a human."

Sketch acknowledged the instructions.

"And you'll choose a human form to transfer into. Think carefully about what shape this will take for you'll inhabit this physical being for the entirety of your time as one of them."

Sketch drew inwards but failed to stop a vibrant surge of light escaping in full view of the One.

"Sketch."

"Yes."

"Your re-admittance to the Core is dependent upon demonstration of an understanding of human needs and how to serve them. No return without learning."

"No return without learning," Sketch repeated.

"Now go," said the One.

As Sketch left, suppressed light under her aura began to disperse around her. Sketch expanded and contracted into free areas of the Core. Moments before, it had been facing the certainty of recycling. Now she was to become a human, a human being like those they observed and served.

Sketch located Inco zoning into an observation of the female human named Jackie. Sat before her PC, she operated the machine with speed, surprising given both her physical age, older humans were not known for their digital dexterity, and the condition of the computer. Jackie turned forty last month and celebrated with alcohol and cake. The experience had a number of ill effects on her ageing body, including pain, nausea, dehydration and a slowing of cognitive functions. Inco and Sketch witnessed this episode of infirmity. Neither of them could understand why humans often choose to do things to fill themselves with pain or induce sadness. Why did they not restrict their activities to those that made them happy or healthy?

"Inco! Inco you'll never guess. You'll just never guess!"

Sketch whizzed around Inco giving off light spores that then gravitated around her orbit.

"If I'll never guess there would be no purpose in me attempting to," he replied.

"Just guess," she said, her spores beginning to spark.

"Can't you just tell me?"

"No!"

Inco projected light in the direction of her being.

"The One awarded you the authority of 10a?"

"No," said Sketch buzzed around Inco.

"Careful. If you vibrate any more you will cause a meltdown in the Core," said Inco. "Slow, stop, and then I think you should tell me the what I will never guess."

"I'm going to be a human, to live with them, to learn." Sketch brightened a little before continuing the effort to contain herself. She pushed the phrase no return without learning away from her thinking. "It's to help me to understand them so I won't continue to make fatal errors."

"I'd guessed from your effervescence you weren't to be recycled," said Inco. "But this type of transformation hasn't occurred since the big human war when they sent out a strategist to aid the Churchill leader."

"Can you imagine it? Me, a human."

"I'm going to feel your absence."

"Why would you miss me? You'll be able to observe me, like we both watch the boy," said Sketch, oblivious to the dimming of her companion. "Oh, I might even meet the boy."

"You'll be amazing. I wish I could come with you," said Inco.

"Really?"

"The human world has much to teach us all."

Sketch beamed.

"Promise me you'll watch as often as is permissible and I'll relay everything to you. Every fact and sensation," she said. "Do you think I should change what I'm known as? I've never heard of a human called Sketch."

"Neither have I, but many of them go by unusual names. Apple, Bear, Blade, Rocket, and Prince are all fitting examples of their erratic naming conventions, so I don't think it will matter. They won't notice a Sketch in their midst, and I like Sketch."

"Then I will stick with Sketch. Will you help me choose my avatar? I don't want to select something inappropriate, and there are so many choices - skin, hair, nose, toes, knees."

"It would lighten me to aid you."

Knowledge flowed through Sketch, filling her with the complex web of information needed to survive outside of the Core in the body of a Homo Sapien. It was designed to give her the basic tools need to undertake her placement. Once in place, it could be accessed both before she transformed and during her stay in the external realm.

"Do you desire to tell me all about the data?" asked Inco.

"The volume of the intelligence is vast. I can't process the flow fast enough. I need time to filter what is important."

The information passed to her was alien to the way she was accustomed to thinking. It held the reality of most things human, from concepts such as colour spectrums to the plots of films dating back to the birth of the moving pictures, detailed descriptions and facts about the moon landings, cultural behaviours and Ronald MacDonald. Sketch attempted to focus on the things she thought would affect her most in the first few days.

"The human I'm going to be living with is a female. She is a single mother with a teenage son who is seventeen. I will also be seventeen," Sketch said, waiting for more information to integrate with her being.

"They live in a place called Tufnell Park, which is in London, to the north of the city. That's where all the buses and the tube trains are situated. No, excuse my error, buses and trains exist all over the world but they are in abundance in the capital of England, part of the United Kingdom of Great Britain and Northern Ireland."

"What about the job? What does it entail?" Inco asked.

"I'm going to work in a library."

"And what is a library?" he said.

"I'd not heard of them before but they are places people go to borrow things and find information. A library is filled with books and films. Real books, not ones you download to a device but rather made up of sheets of paper and beautiful printed covers. I'm going to be a volunteer assistant at the Northgate Central South library in Kentish Town. It will be part of what they call 'work experience' for young people, to aid in their education."

"Where is Kentish Town?"

"It's just down the road from Tufnell Park, in the borough of Northgate. Places are bigger than I imagined they'd be in the external realm. Space is an unusual concept. The humans travel through it in a very different way to us."

The data transfer revealed that the woman, whilst being a human, was also a liaison between worlds. Her ability to read auras led to her recruitment to assist with transformations to and from the Core and to communicate vital sources of data otherwise hidden from the internal realm. Sketch had been instructed not to share this information. To do so would lead to recycling. It was challenging not to tell Inco, but being trusted with a secret added to her sense of importance.

"It's all stimulating and to no small extent enlivening, but I'll miss you," said Inco. "It will be…duller in here without you."

"Time will pass quickly. You'll not perceive my absence," said Sketch. "You can hang out with the qualifieds stationed near you instead of wasting your time struggling to help me."

"Sketch… there's something I need to tell you."

"Oh, and at the library, I get to teach people how to use the computer. Amazing."

Inco's attempts to communicate went unnoticed by Sketch, nor did she detect his aura fading to a shadow of her own.

"When are you going to transform?" Inco asked, focusing back on Sketch's form.

"It's scheduled for about an hour from now. Will you be here to wave me off? That's what humans say when someone leaves for a journey."

Sketch glowed, proud of her new knowledge.

"Of course I will."

INCO WAS NOT the only one present to observe the transformation of Sketch. The rarity of the event attracted a swarm of energies. Intense curiosity, excitement and a little envy existed amongst them.

The One stilled the raucous vibrations in the Core with an atmospheric dispersal, forcing everyone to become stationary.

"We send Sketch to another realm. She will live as a human, she will experience the joys and frustrations of a complex life in a different, unpredictable form, and she will learn all she needs to be able to return to us and become qualified," The One said before a heavy pause. "Or she will not return."

Sketch fizzled with a combination of chromatic arousal at the forthcoming challenge and a rising sense of agitation.

"The human realm is not without dangers, but from our place of safety inside the Core we have learnt about many of them. Sketch," it said, turning its address from the assembled energies to the young one beside it. "You have been given an opportunity to affect not only yourself, but others in a realm where three dimensions are all that are acknowledged. Go forward and learn. Learn and return."

The crowd surged in concurrence, a pulse of "learn and return" building to a crescendo.

Sketch began to expand. What had she agreed to? Wouldn't it be better to stay? She observed the form of Inco and sensed everything would be okay because he was there. She pulled her light energy together in readiness for the dispersal process, reminding herself it was this or a recycling. All remaining vibrations stilled to a halt as The One boomed out a countdown.

"Ten, nine, eight, seven, six…" The counting grew louder and more forceful as the energies within the Core came together as one, mobilising their combined power. "Five, four, three, two, one."

The auras surrounding Sketch began to pixelate and fade, gradually at first and then at speed, disappearing into a black, shrinking tunnel before becoming visible only as a pinprick of light. In a nanosecond, it blinked out of sight.

Pure darkness took control of the space around her as Sketch entered the process of transformation from a light-infused computer energy to a living, air-breathing human, aged seventeen years old and able to walk around in the world outside of the computer.

The Human World

Chapter 2

SKETCH REACHED the other side and emerged, atom by atom into the living room of her human host. It was a disorientating process like the dizzying, stomach-churning spinning that occurs when the body is wrenched in all directions by the twists and turns of a roller-coaster. Upon transforming, Sketch threw up on the faded green patterned carpet and collapsed sideways onto a conveniently located old leather sofa.

"Bloody hell," said the woman. "Either this is really happening or the little white men in coats will be knocking on my door before we know it." She rubbed her eyes and pinched her arm.

Coming around, Sketch felt the weight of her body. How could it be so heavy and feel so light and lacking substance at the same time? She held up her arm, examining its length, touching it from shoulder to finger tips with her other hand. It was solid and warm. The layer encasing the unseen parts of her anatomy was soft, smooth and covered with a fine, fair layer of hair. She pulled at the downy strands, puckering up the skin below and then released them. Each hair returned to its former position.

Sketch attempted to move from the sofa but she wobbled and the nausea returned, forcing her to return to her seat.

"Don't try to get up, hon. Your muscles aren't strong enough yet. Just sit still while I get you a hot cuppa. My name's Jackie, by the way." She smiled at Sketch and walked through to the kitchen. A small hatch in a partition wall divided the two rooms, allowing the pair to view each other from their respective areas.

Jackie appeared brighter to Sketch on this side than she had from behind the ageing screen of the computer. Sketch raised her nose upwards and sniffed, smelling the toasty air from the room's radiators, traces of Jackie's perfume and the scent of flowers sat too long in stagnant water. The matching swirling motion in her tummy and head continued to occur when she tried movement, so she took Jackie's advice and stayed still, her body in contact with the safety of the sofa. She took hold of a cushion, hugging it close to her stomach whilst exploring the contrast between her fingers and the malleable material. She raised it up, level with her head.

It's pink, Sketch thought to herself. The Core operated by light and darkness alone, absent of colour except for the blue screen of death which occurred alongside a fatal error. The concept she'd learnt about from the data transfer was nothing when faced with the myriad of pigments, tints and shades now assaulting her eyes. Her voice also came as a surprise, different to many of the voices she'd translated to pulses from the Internet or through the screen, but she liked it and it seemed to be an excellent match to her new appearance.

I sound young. Bubbly but not squeaky, she thought. *This is good, no one wants to be squeaky.*

"Here you go, hon. Drink this. I've put a couple sugars in it to give you a bit of extra energy," said Jackie, passing over a cup of steaming hot tea.

Sketch's brain processed the writing on the mug as BT, a communications company that owns all the landlines on the telephone network. This wasn't a new fact for her as the broadband links into the computer came from this source.

"Careful now. Just sip at it. It's hot. You don't want to scald your tongue."

"It's pleasant."

Jackie laughed. "I've not heard it called that before."

From her vantage point on the cream flower-patterned sofa, Sketch surveyed the room. Photos, plants and books of differing sizes and colours populated the space. The furniture, adorned by throws and cushions created a welcoming, lived in atmosphere. Two sofas sat opposite each other, allowing plenty of room for visitors to sit in comfort. In one corner, near a pair of packed bookcases, was a piano covered with papers, bank statements, envelopes and birthday cards. Across from where Sketch sat hung an oblong mirror etched with a picture of a nymph-like woman.

"Oh," she said, seeing herself for the first time. "White spiky hair…and metal things in my face. Like I asked for. I have a face."

Jackie smiled as Sketch turned towards her, mouth open and piercing green eyes shining.

"We say 'blonde'. The colour of your hair is blonde, that is. It suits you," Jackie said.

To the other side of the room, divided by bookcases and their adorning ornaments, was a sizeable wooden dining table capable of seating twelve people.

"This must all be a bit weird for you," said Jackie. "God knows I'm having problems getting my head round it."

Sketch nodded and raised a small smile, testing out the sensation of turning up the muscles around her lips.

"Don't worry. We've got all day tomorrow to get you settled in and finding your feet…and your arms and your head," Jackie told Sketch, laughing at her own joke.

The two strangers sat in the same room, neither speaking, when a series of loud noises, a whizzing and whirling followed by a bang, bang, bang, clap, rang out. Sketch jolted upright, looking around in every direction on high alert like a wild animal sensing danger. She couldn't see anything or locate where the alarming noises were coming from. She scoured through the contents of the data transfer, but some of it had vanished. She clamped her hands over her ears and screamed.

Jackie rushed to her, making soothing noises in a gentle voice. She gathered Sketch up in her arms and held her tight.

"It's ok. It's just fireworks, nothing to worry about. We have them every year about this time. Come and see," said the older woman. Jackie led Sketch to a window, pulled the velvet green curtains aside and revealing the dark sky outside. The pitch black of the night was tinged by the hazy glow of artificial lighting from buildings and street lamps littering the city. Against the urban backdrop flew dazzling sparkles of coloured lights, roaring into the expanse of the evening sky before fizzling out or falling downwards toward the ground.

"They're so beautiful." The sound of the fireworks pierced Sketch's ears and the light show imprinted images upon her eyes through the glass. "Why do they make such an ugly sound?" asked Sketch.

"Never thought of that before. They need the noise to launch into the air. Inside their casings is a mixture of chemicals used to shoot them into the sky and explode."

Sketch laughed. "You know they remind me of something, in the computer."

I can't wait to tell Inco about these magical lights, she thought, smiling to herself. *They are so like activated energies but with colours.*

Being in the human world would be okay with the bright lights of her reality just outside the window.

"What are they for? Is everyone excited?"

Jackie began to explain about the fifth of November and the story of Guy Fawkes, the Catholic who tried to blow up the House of Parliament in the Gunpowder Plot. Since sixteen hundred and five, the failure of the plot had been celebrated with the burning of a make-believe Guy made of stuffed clothes.

"And that's when fireworks started?" asked Sketch.

Jackie paused. "All this must seem very peculiar to you, and to be fair, hon, it is a bit odd. We stole the idea of fireworks from the Chinese. They were using them for years before we thought of getting in on the act."

Sketch moved back to the sofa, confused about why people would steal things from each other.

"So, where is your son? Is he out with his friends? What's he called?"

"No, I've sent him to his dad's tonight. God knows he should spend more blooming time with him. I thought I'd get you settled in and then you can meet him tomorrow night."

"Thank you," said Sketch feeling able to slump back down again.

"Oh, and his name's Matt."

Sketch jerked upward, blood rushing through her body. This was the home of Jackie and Matt, human users of the computer serviced by the Core. She would be living in the house of the boy Matt. Trying to hide her heightened sense of agitation she searched around the room, her eyes falling on the computer. It sat squashed in a corner of the room. Sketch stared at the machine, wondering if Inco and the other energies from the Core were watching her.

"Do you want to go on it?" Jackie asked her, noticing where he eyes had landed.

Sketch nodded. "Can I?"

"It's very slow so it'll take an age to warm up."

"I know."

"Of course you do. Silly me."

"It might work better without me in it," said Sketch, head downwards as if studying the outdated pattern on the carpet.

"Rubbish," said Jackie. "Why don't you turn it on and we'll watch TV 'til it's ready?" Jackie plugged in the TV set. "I don't like to leave it on standby, bad for the environment."

"The television is run by energies, too."

"Is it now? There's such a lot we don't understand. Speaking of which, it's important you know a bit about what's on television. You won't stand out as much if you can chat about what's been on to people."

They settled down to watch a segment of a talent show.

"It's a big singing contest with judges in the studio. We can vote for the ones we like the best with our phones," said Jackie.

Sketch didn't think there was much talent involved and the

judges seemed more intent on outdoing one another with barbed comments but she kept her thoughts to herself.

"Thanks, Jackie. I want to learn everything," she said.

"Think the computer should be good to go now if you still want to use it."

"Oh yes, thank you."

Sketch sat in front of the PC.

"Hello," she said in a whisper. She peeked over her shoulder at Jackie, whose attention was focused on the TV screen. Assured no one in this world could see what she was typing, she entered the URL for Matt's anonymous blog, Teen about Town. A new post, written ten minutes ago, held top position on the page.

It seems unfair that at the age of seventeen I can have sex, drive a car and join the army, but I'm still forced, by my mum, to spend Saturday night with my dad and his near-teenaged girlfriend.

Dad calls M his partner but she's so young that makes it sound like they are at school working on a lab assignment together. Tonight, they're all cosy-cosy and I'm trapped in the same room as they watch bloody crap on the telly.

"I know you teenagers like The X Factor,*" he said. "But we're totally hooked on* Strictly, *aren't we M?" It's as if they're retired and nearly dead. Never ever will I allow myself to become like them. They're a cautionary tale to all teens.*

Still, being at Dad's is better than being at home. Mum is having one of her hippy friends over. She's been making up the office into a spare room. Mum's a bit prone to bringing home waifs and strays so there's a pretty decent sofa bed in there. Earlier I found her adding weird knick-knacks and copies of Spirit and Destiny *magazine to the reading material at the side of the sofa. That's a sure sign it's one of those floaty, dippy types. I shudder to think. The only way through is to plug my iPod into my tortured ears and check my notifications like all the other disillusioned teens.*

Sketch read Matt's blog twice before logging off without commenting.

I'm neither floaty nor dippy, she thought. *Am I?*

"Are you alright, hon?" asked Jackie from her seat across the room. The talent show had finished and the television was churning out adverts.

"Uh, I'm a bit…I feel funny," Sketch replied. "Heavy, puffy, like someone's removed my human battery." She found herself beginning to fade, drained and unable to take in any more information.

"You're exhausted."

Jackie led Sketch up a flight of stairs to the ground floor where her bedroom and the bathroom were. The sofa bed was made up with crisp white sheets and a lilac covered feather duvet and matching pillows. Jackie also provided Sketch with clothing, including sleepwear.

"They'll keep you cosy now that the heating's gone off," said Jackie. "I'll show you the bathroom and about brushing your teeth. Do it twice a day, mind, and everything'll be fine."

After basic instruction in the workings of the bathroom, Jackie made to leave Sketch to settle in for the night.

"Sleep tight, Sketch. I'm just along the hall if you need me. And if you get up before me tomorrow, just rummage around until you find what you need."

"Night, Jackie. And thank you."

Crawling into her bed awarded her the new sensation of being covered by the duvet. She grinned in contentment. The inner glow Sketch felt, she would soon come to recognize as human happiness. She drifted off to sleep for the first time.

Chapter 3

SKETCH SLEPT without any dreams that she could recall, awaking at the sound of knocking on the bedroom door. She rubbed her eyes and remembered she was in a house in the human world.

"Wakey, wakey, rise and shiny," said Jackie, entering before any response.

Sketch opened one eye and shut it again. Sleep was nice, delightful, and she wanted more.

"No, Sketch. I'm afraid we've got a lot to cover today if you want to be ready for tomorrow," said Jackie holding her ground.

Sketch failed to move. Jackie whipped the bedding away from her. She groaned, reopened her eyes and began the painful process of waking up.

"You're lucky I didn't pour cold water on you. Been tempted to do that to Matt on occasion," said Jackie, laughing. "You'll need to get dressed and wrap up warm 'cause we're heading out."

"Out?"

"We aren't going far," Jackie assured her. "Just around the corner to a café for breakfast. You'll be wanting to put on a hat and scarf. It's freezing today."

Bundled up, Sketch still felt the chill of the late autumn air and pulled her coat and woollies around her, covering up as much of her skin as possible as they left the flat. She gazed up at the clear winter sky as sounds of traffic, footfalls and an overhead plane reached her ears. Things were different outside of the Townsend's house.

"This trip is just to help you get your bearings," said Jackie. "That way you don't get lost tomorrow on the way to the library. Come on, let's get some food."

There was one other person in the café aside from the girl behind the counter. A man sat eating a breakfast of fried eggs, bacon, mushrooms, sausage, baked beans and hash browns smothered with tomato sauce. Sketch found the combined aroma of meat and grease appealing.

"I want one of those," she said pointing to the man's food. Her face resembled a hungry dog, ready to pounce upon his plate and run off with his remaining sausage.

"You can choose what you like. That's what we call a full English. This kind of breakfast is tasty but not so good for your body so we don't eat them all the time. They're more like special treats for weekends."

The amazing food was all Sketch could think of as she tore into a sausage with her knife and fork. The flavour of the meat as it connected with her tongue was startling. She moved her jaws up and down in quick succession, shoveling the breakfast into her mouth for the start of its journey down through her digestive system.

"You might want to slow down a little, Sketch. You'll enjoy it even more that way," said Jackie.

Sketch began to pace herself and found Jackie had a point. The flavours oozed out increasing the saliva in her mouth.

"This world is good!" said Sketch in between mouthfuls.

The café wasn't a trendy coffee shop, with writers, yummy mummies, and freshly ground coffee, nor was it a greasy spoon. The menus were traditional but touches, such as quirky tea pots, comfy chairs and the occasional potted plants, gave the illusion of it being someone's living room rather than a café. Sketch thought the woman serving and cooking provided an adequate demonstration of the human ability to multi-task but she had some difficulties in understanding Jackie when she was asked for a "decaf" tea.

"Poor love," said Jackie after the waitress had gone. "Must be difficult when your English isn't that good."

"There are lots of different languages spoken in London, aren't there? I know that from my data transfer," said Sketch.

"Plenty. People from all over the world live here," Jackie replied, finishing up the dregs of her tea. "I thought it would be helpful for us to take a walk down the road to show you where Northgate Central South Library is."

Sketch nodded, zipping up her coat. After paying the bill, they exited the café and turned left onto Fortess Road. They passed a procession of shops selling everything from fruit and vegetables, to artefacts from Africa, clothes, and household items. The street featured many places to dine out and buy ready-cooked meals to eat at home. There was also a range of services establishments including a hairdresser, insurance company, a launderette and an undertaker for assisting the process of transformation when humans die.

"Jackie? Why do people need to leave here?"

Jackie stopped and regarded Sketch. "What do you mean?"

"Well, everything a human would need for survival is here on this street. Why does anyone go any further?"

"Us humans are a curious type. People like to explore a new area, to make friends from other places but I think it's also got a lot to do with buying things."

"Why?" Jackie's answer didn't make any sense to Sketch.

"All around us people are trying to persuade us to spend money. Even if we've got a perfectly good computer they want us to buy a newer one," said Jackie, sighing. "It's all the advertising that does it, impossible to get through a day without seeing ads. They are everywhere, just everywhere."

Sketch listened as Jackie went on to describe the types of things people thought they had to own to mark their status in society. Without the right icons, people would be laughed at, seen as behind the times or stupid.

"Me, I'll try and fix things. Keep them going as long as possible. It's dead easy to get spare parts for stuff now that we've got the Internet. Matt, well he's another kettle of fish."

"A kettle of fish?" asked Sketch.

"Just one of those things we say. It's his friends. Their parents give them everything and they tease him for not having them, too. I want him to get a job and save up for things. It's too easy for me just to give them to him," said Jackie. "Thing is, it's a bit hard right now. There aren't the same jobs around for teenagers there were a few years ago but I'm sure he uses that as an excuse to not even look for one."

It was still early for a Sunday and there were few people around despite the temperature being mild for the time of year. A number of runners passed the two women by, making exercise look effortless. Jackie moved out of the way whenever she saw one coming.

"Tried jogging once," she said. "Nearly killed me by the time I'd got to the Heath. No idea how I got back."

At the bottom of the road was a major junction, with roads leading to Kentish Town, Camden, Highgate, and Hampstead Heath. The pair continued on their path until they crossed the street to the tube station. Sketch's face lit up.

"Are we going on the underground?"

"I'm afraid not. The library is close to here but we can go on the tube later if you like. Just so you can see what it's like."

"Brilliant," said Sketch, a giant toothy grin lighting up her face.

The library was situated next to Jayne's, a florist bringing beautiful blooms to the area of North London.

"Here we are," said Jackie. "It's closed on a Sunday but we can look inside from here."

Sketch peered through the big glass-fronted window. From their position on the pavement, she could see a display about knitting comprising of a number of books, knitting needles and some examples of what it should look like when the wool had been manipulated into patterns. To the right, she spotted a section for children and in the distance, Sketch saw shelves filled with books. The area closest to the window had rectangular tables and a hot drinks machine.

"That bit's like a little café. It's the only part of the library where you can eat or have a cuppa. People come here to read the newspapers or just to sit and use the free Wi-Fi," said Jackie. "There's also a lot of people who go to the library 'cause it's warm in there, particularly the older ones."

"Is it cold in their homes?"

"Many people don't have enough money to keep the heating on in their houses, even in the winter when they need it most."

"That's sad. So, what will I be doing here?" asked Sketch, changing the subject.

"They'll give you all the details when you arrive tomorrow but you'll be helping people to find information with books and teaching them to use the computers."

"I hope I can do it," mumbled Sketch. Jackie didn't hear her but spotted the downcast expression on her face.

"Come on. Let's take that tube ride back to Tufnell Park."

Jackie dipped into her bag and brought out a small black plastic case which held an oyster card, a credit card sized rectangle that allowed its user to sign in and out of the capital's public transport system.

"It's pre-paid with a travel card for zones one and two for the next month."

Sketch turned it over and over in her hands. This little rectangle of plastic meant she could explore the city.

"Make sure you don't lose it, though. I wouldn't want you getting stuck in some strange part of London," said Jackie.

"Oh don't worry, I'll guard it with my life," said Sketch.

Jackie led Sketch through the barriers and down the escalator. Sketch thought about all the energies contributing to making the moving staircase take people down into the underground space. Reaching the platform, they found a seat and waited for a train to High Barnet due to arrive in five minutes' time.

"At rush hour, when people are travelling to work, there are more trains. But on a Sunday, we'll be waiting longer," said Jackie.

Sketch didn't mind waiting. She would be happy to sit on the platform all day, absorbing the sounds and smells of the underground. The air in the tube station smelt different than the air on the street, in the café or even the rooms in Jackie's house. It sent dirty metallic odours into Sketch's nostrils, making her sniff in curiosity. Adding to the distinctive smells were the scents of the people waiting to board the train. From sweat to perfumes and pasties, the platform seemed awash with the aroma of human life.

As they waited, Jackie showed Sketch the underground map and pointed to their destination. "The map isn't to scale. It's just to help you get around. The gaps between stops vary a lot, but there's always an announcement to tell you when to get off."

The train pulled into the station and they allowed the departing passengers to get off. An old woman, in her late seventies, wearing a purple fur trimmed coat, struggled to get off with her shopping trolley. Jackie stepped in to lend a hand before boarding the carriage with Sketch.

"Poor soul. I can't imagine what it must be like to be that age, doing your weekly shop. I hope I've got some family around to take me out when I get to that stage," said Jackie, taking a seat next to Sketch.

The excitement of being on a tube train and hearing the announcement, "This is a Northern Line train to High Barnet; the next station is Tufnell Park," made Sketch forget about the old lady in the purple coat. She fell in love with the tube's patterned upholstery, adverts and maps, and was somewhat put out when Jackie forced her to alight a minute later.

Unlike at Kentish Town, Tufnell Park station had two lifts by which passengers exited to the ground floor. Today however, both lifts had malfunctioned at the same time.

"Are we stuck?" asked Sketch hoping they could get another tube back to Kentish Town and walk home from there.

"Nope, there's a spiral staircase that takes you to the top. It's either that or hang on for an engineer, but we could wait weeks for one of them."

They began the climb. Sketch gripped the railing to secure herself.

"Are we nearly there yet?" she panted as they reached stair number seventy-three.

Jackie laughed between breaths. "You sound like a little kid. Well, I suppose you are. It's all so new to you. Yes, just around the corner now."

On returning to the house Jackie turned on the TV and activated the central heating.

We'll just grab a cuppa and then I'll go through some of the other things you need to know. Most of them you should have from the data...what's it called?" she said, poking her head through the hatch.

"Data transfer," said Sketch. "I've lost some of it."

"Best we double check then."

Sketch realised that having a hot drink was an important ritual for humans but also a rather pleasant thing to do. She followed Jackie to the kitchen, watching her prepare the drinks. Next time she would make the teas.

"I've got you some things you'll need here," said Jackie, handing Sketch a mustard coloured rucksack.

Inside Sketch found a mobile phone, notebook, pens, a purse with some money, tissues, a hair brush, a packet of breath mints, and a small makeup bag containing lipstick, blusher, eyeliner, eyeshadow, and mascara.

"The mobile's one of them smartphone things, a refurbished model. Cost a fortune new, they do, and Matt's already broken one this year."

Sketch examined the phone. It was an old Sony. Despite its age, she would still be able to text, call people, take photos and, with a little effort, access the Internet and install apps for social media. She played around with it for a bit, working out how the phone functioned and customising it, where possible, to what she thought would be of greatest utility.

Next, she tried putting on makeup but with less success. She ended up both looking and feeling a little like a clown.

"Good attempt," said Jackie trying to be positive about Sketch's first go with cosmetics. "You might want to look for tips on the Internet because I'm not very good with makeup myself."

"I suppose."

"It'd be best to get on the computer before Matt gets home."

The PC took a little while to start up as it had been shut down after Sketch's session the night before.

"I'm always telling Matt to turn it off when he's finished. It's so much better for the environment," said Jackie.

Sketch knew from her time observing Matt from the Core that, like many teenagers he had ignoring his parents down to a fine art—he never shutdown the computer.

Sketch smiled and whispered to the screen. "Hi, it's me… Sketch." If Inco wasn't in operation he would be observing her.

"It's amazing here. I've been on the tube, eaten sausages. Sausages are amazing. The boy Matt is coming home soon and I'm a bit nervous…"

She tailed off knowing that whatever she said Inco couldn't reply.

"I've been learning about the humans; they are complicated..."

The front door of the Townsend abode opened and closed announcing the arrival of the boy Matt.

"Mum, I'm home," came a deep voice from the floor above.

"We're down here, hon."

Sketch turned around from the computer screen and watched as Matt blundered into the basement living room. His feet and legs appearing first, followed by his torso and finally his familiar head and shoulders. He was taller than his mum at six foot one. His dark hair swept across his forehead like a photo of a wave frozen in a fixed point of time.

"You're back early," said Jackie.

Matt shrugged. "Stuff to do and I couldn't be bothered with dad and Molly making lovesick eyes at one another. Who's this then?" he asked, looking over at Sketch and then back at Jackie.

"This is Sketch. Remember I told you she's going to be staying with us for a few weeks. I'm going to need you to show her around the area as she's not from London."

Matt looked at Sketch. "Don't remember but yeh, alright."

"Thank you, Matt," said Jackie, relieved he hadn't ask any more questions about where their visitor had come from.

"Can I get on the computer to check stuff? The battery's dead on my iPod and my phone's got no apps. Can you believe that?" Matt complained.

"That's because you broke the one your dad got you for Christmas," Jackie replied.

Sketch moved away from the computer. "It's all yours. Nice to meet you, Matt," she said trying to sound normal as her stomach churned and her cheeks warmed.

"Yeh, you too."

Matt's attention was gone.

"Don't worry Sketch. It's not you. The moment he gets on the computer I can't get a word out of him, same with the telly. It'd take a bomb to move him."

Sketch didn't mind. Being in the same room as Matt was enough. He was even more beautiful in real life; young, strong and sociable. She could tell the latter by his need to get onto the Internet as soon as he got back. It must be to chat with his friends. She'd sent friend requests to Matt and Jackie on as many social media sites she could find so in no time at all he would be her friend, too.

She kept glancing over to the computer when she thought Jackie wasn't looking.

"I always jump in when Matt's not there, otherwise I don't get a look in," said Jackie. She turned on the TV and switched to the Songs of Praise. "Sometimes the singing of hymns drives him to his room," she added.

This time Jackie's tactics failed to shift Matt from the computer but Sketch enjoyed viewing him from the outside of the Core. She lasted until nine thirty before a compelling urge to sleep took control of her body. She was on the verge of nodding off on the sofa, her eyes heavy and mind at a standstill.

"I think it's time you took yourself up the stairs to Bedfordshire," said Jackie.

"Bedfordshire is upstairs?" asked Sketch, somewhat confused despite referring to her data download.

"It's just one of those silly sayings we have," said Jackie. "It just means bed. Have you got everything you need?"

"Yes," Sketch replied, with a nod and a yawn. She pulled herself from the comfort of the sofa, overwhelmed by the effects of gravity on her physical body and headed up to her room.

❄

LYING IN BED, Sketch fidgeted. Her insides wiggled around as if hosting the contents of a wormery. So far, living as a human had been easy, but tomorrow was full of unknowns: an unknown job, unknown people, unknown dangers and challenges. What if she couldn't do it? The word of the One lurked in corners in her head, jumping out to taunt her. "No return without learning. No return without learning. No return with learning."

Sketch shook herself. *This is the wrong attitude to have*, she thought. *I must be more positive, but what if the One sent me here knowing I would fail?*

Anxiety and nervousness kept her awake into the early hours of the following day. It was only after she'd given up all attempts to sleep did Sketch finally drift off into unconsciousness.

Chapter 4

DESPITE BEING FOREWARNED that sausages were not on the breakfast menu on a Monday morning, Sketch screwed her face up when presented with a plate of bran flakes. She was less than impressed with their taste. Even a slice of chunky toast didn't make it any better. In comparison to her first day's full English, they tasted bland and functional. She sat at the dining room table spooning the cereal into her mouth when Matt came downstairs in his school uniform and grabbed some toast from the metal rack on the kitchen table.

"Mum force feeding you healthy gunk?" he asked, gesturing towards the soggy cereal.

"Yeh," said Sketch. "She wouldn't let me have sausages."

"Not on a weekday." Matt grinned. Sketch felt her body fill with a liquid warmth akin to sunlight. Matt thought the same things as her. Things about the amazingness of sausages, at that.

"If you nip into the café on the way to the library, you can get a sausage sandwich before you start. Or there's a Greggs down the road. Get one there."

"Thanks, Matt. I might just do that."

Sketch wasn't sure what a Greggs was but thought it best not to ask. Aside from a disappointing breakfast and her lack of sleep, she felt the day had begun well.

"Shall I walk with you?" asked Sketch as Matt piled books and sports shoes into a bag.

"Thanks, but I'm going the opposite way and school starts way earlier than libraries. You're lucky to be doing work experience."

"Ok, see you later, unless you're off to meet friends."

"Err, yeh. See you," said Matt dashing out the door with another slice of toast between his teeth.

Jackie made up a packed lunch for Sketch, including some sandwiches filled with egg on wholemeal bread, an apple, a banana, and a flapjack.

"It's homemade bread I baked before you arrived," Jackie told her.

With the food bundled into her bag alongside her phone, money and door keys, Sketch set off for her first day of work experience. It didn't take long for her to spot the Greggs and she decided to head there first. She stepped into the shop and purchased a sausage in a crusty bread roll with extra ketchup, before scooting between stationary cars while the traffic was caught up in rush hour gridlock. She nipped behind a 134 bus, destined for Tottenham Court Road, smiling as she sauntered into the library, sausage sarnie in hand.

"Stop!" shouted a voice from nowhere. Sketch froze.

"Put down the sausage," said the voice. Sketch identified it as coming from behind a man-sized bookcase halfway across the room. She looked at the bread encased sausage and then around her but could see no place to place the offending item. Was it illegal to eat sausages on a weekday? At what seemed like rapid speed, the hidden voice turned into a person standing beside Sketch with her hand stretched out in front of her.

"Hand it over," the woman demanded.

Sketch panicked and placed the sausage straight into her hands.

"I'm sorry."

"I should think so. Food is banned in the library and I've got a bit of a sore head. The official cure for it is a sausage sandwich."

The dark haired woman took a chunky bite into Sketch's butty before handed it back. "Finish it quick then before I nick the rest."

"You must be Sketch. I'm Begw, Begw Jones." She continued holding out her hand, this time for a shake and not for a sausage. Sketch shook hands. She couldn't speak because her mouth was engaged in the task of trying to eat the remainder of the sandwich in one go, scared the loud woman would take it off her again.

"Have you ever been in a library before? Young people often haven't." Sketch opened her mouth to say she looked about the same age as Begw but found it still full of food. She shook her head.

"Suppose I better show you the basics then and afterwards I'll introduce you to Trevor."

Begw was small at five foot two but seemed to be much taller. Her confident, forthright manner made Sketch feel shorter and a bit unsettled. Her long, dark hair had a spirit level straight fringe. The pair walked through shelves of books, passing by some racks of CDs and the designated youth area towards the back of the room.

"This is the most important place in the library," said Begw, opening a door emblazoned with STAFF ONLY in bold, black lettering. Through the door was the staffroom with its own teeny kitchen.

"Time for a *panad*," announced Begw.

"Oh, I can make tea," said Sketch, eager to impress her new boss.

"You speak Welsh? Are you from North Wales?" said Begw, her eyebrows raised towards her fringe.

Sketch realised that although the data transfer gave her the ability to understand hundreds of languages, it had stopped halfway. She had no knowledge of how to speak or write any of them.

"Er no, but I know a few words," said Sketch. She knew lying was bad, but this was more a twisting of the truth, so she thought it would be okay. "Just *panad* and *popty ping*."

"Cool," said Begw. "I'll have a tea with one sugar and half a teaspoon of milk. Just half a spoon, mind–I can tell the difference."

Begw sat and played with the Facebook app on her iPhone as Sketch made them both hot drinks.

"You've not many friends on Facebook, do you Sketch? I'll be your friend. We can't be having lonely people here. It'll all help when you're showing the oldies what to do."

Another friend, thought Sketch with a growing sense of confidence.

After their hot drinks, Begw showed Sketch around the library. As they exited the staff room, there was a flat screen TV mounted to the wall. Its purpose was to show notices about getting help with employment and training. It also advertised some of the courses Sketch would be teaching to the older humans.

"Silver Surfers, that's one of yours," Begw said as they walked past the TV. It flashed up images of people sending emails, with beaming faces and airbrushed grey or white hair. Other areas displayed showed different posters for a range of groups, activities and support services. Snaking between the aisles of books from horror to romance a la Mills and Boon, they reached Teenspace, an area of the library dedicated to young people with selected notices, information, books and three computers set aside for use by people under twenty-five.

"Does that mean we have to ask the man to leave?" asked Sketch, noticing a pensioner sat looking at a blank screen as if something was about to happen. He was definitely over twenty-five and Sketch was scared of the possible consequences if she broke any of the rules.

"Nope, that's just Mr Barrington. He gets confused."

Begw turned to the man with white hair and a matching beard. "Come on now, Mr Barrington. It's not Silver Surfers 'til tomorrow. You can come and see the lovely Sketch then."

He nodded, smiled at them both and shuffled off.

"Sorry, Miss Jones."

"Not a problem, Mr Barrington. And you can call me Begw." She whispered to Sketch, "He can't pronounce my name so he calls me Miss Jones. Not many people can. There's this annoying woman with fuzzy hair, who calls me Bigwee," she said sighing.

A large desk with the lime green plastic trim, stationed in the middle of the library, was the hub of operations. It hosted the staff computer.

"We use this to run queries for members who came looking for books we don't have in," said Begw. "We stock a limited number of books. With all the cuts in services by the council this past year, we're lucky to still be here. If Camden, Islington and Haringey boroughs hadn't merged to form the Northgate super council, I think we'd be gone. It's important we still cater to the old people like Mr Barrington. Coming in here's like going to the post office for them. They come for a natter. Without us, they might not speak to another soul for days."

Sketch looked around the library and noticed Begw was right. The majority of the people appeared to be over the age of seventy, white hair, and the occasional blue rinse, giving them away.

"You don't see many of them hairdos anymore," said Begw. "That's Dora, the blue one. Lovely old lady, but she's a bit dotty and sometimes thinks I'm her granddaughter."

Dora stood in the romance section.

"I let her believe it. No harm done. She buys me Turkish Delight for Christmas and I always make sure there's a Mills and Boon on hand for her."

"Begw..." Sketch began.

"Yup," the other woman replied.

"The elderly people, like Dora and Mr...err..."

"Mr Barrington?"

"Yes. Won't learning to use the computer be a bit…much for them?" Sketch asked.

"No, they're not all like that. Some are dead quick. Smart, you know? And they love the Silver Surfers course once they get going on it," her boss replied. "Anyway, they've got a brilliant teacher now, haven't they?"

Sketch blushed and managed to mumble a "yes".

Begw handed Sketch a slip of paper.

"It's the staff login for all the computers. Keep. It. Safe." she said raising her eyebrows and stretching her face as she spoke.

"Don't worry. I will."

"Best memorise it and eat it."

Sketch looked down at the paper and the complicated password and placed it on her tongue.

"Oh, for goodness sake. I was joking," said Begw with a sigh. "Youth of today. Suppose at least you'll know what to do with the computers."

Sketch laughed. "Yeh, I guess I'll be okay."

Sketch's first morning went quickly. With so many things to remember, she juggled the information around in her brain, trying to work out which bits were the most important and which she could discard. She'd learnt about the different classes on offer, and she could give informed answers to members about how to order books, CDs and DVDs held in other branches.

Begw smiled when Sketch made her more tea and shared her lunch.

"Can't beat a good sarnie," said Begw, throwing away the crusts from one of Sketch's sandwiches. "You didn't want that last one, did you?"

Sketch shook her head. "Shall I go back to stacking shelves again?"

"We can do better than that," Begw told her. "It's story time this afternoon. You can sit in with Trevor and make sure the children don't eat him."

Begw led Sketch through to the children's library where Trevor sat leafing through picture books. To Sketch's eyes, he was tall and skinny, as if he'd forgotten to eat for a couple of weeks.

"Oh Sketch, that's a name and a half. Liking it. And that hair of yours is divine. Isn't it funky, B?"

"Yeh, it's alright. Can't beat a good, straight fringe," replied the Library Manager.

"Lucky you've got enough for a fringe," said Trevor running his clean trimmed fingernails through his thinning hair. He sighed.

"I'll leave you to it," said Begw.

Trevor took Sketch by the arm and led her over to children's non-fiction.

"Let's you and me have a chat. Seats are comfier over here. They're a bit bigger than over in picture books."

Sketch squeezed herself down onto a cushioned ladybird stool, wiggling in an attempt to find a good spot to rest but finding none.

"Begw tells me you're staying with Jackie Townsend. Good woman. Must be strange for you being away from home."

"Err, yes it is, very strange. Will there be many children today?"

"A few but don't worry, it's easy and today you'll just be watching today."

"Today?" asked Sketch. She still had to master working behind the counter, checking in and out books for members. She also had her classes to think about. That was enough.

"If you like it, you can have a go at telling the stories next week. Do you have a boyfriend?"

"What?" Sketch looked up, mouth agog, heart racing. What did this have to do with story time?

"You know, a nice boy to spoil you?"

"Errm, no." Her cheeks became inflamed. Why was he asking her this?

"There is someone I like," she said, her voice reduced to a mumble.

Trevor leant in closer. She wished she could grab back her words, shove them back into her mouth.

"Ohhhhhh, tell me all about him."

Sketch sighed. He seemed interested but she wasn't sure if she should start talking to someone about her feelings.

"His name is Matt. We've only just met but I feel like I've known him for years. It's complicated."

"It always is, lovely, it always is," said Trevor with a dramatic sigh. "I prefer older men myself. More likely to know what they want. This Matt, does he know how you feel?"

"Not yet, but I think he likes me. We have lots in common."

"Look at you in a daydream, getting all mushy over some boy. Careful or we'll be calling you Mushy," said Trevor. Sketch's face began to show repeated signs of embarrassment.

"I'm just teasing you. Blimey, you are a sensitive one."

Unsure what to think, Sketch smiled at Trevor, hoping that would be enough to change the subject.

The children's library was spacious enough for pushchairs, parents and the occasional nappy change. A glass wall separated it from the rest of the library, designed to stop children from wandering off and to aid staff in making sure no harm came to the small humans. No food was allowed in the library. Begw and Trevor tried to enforce this rule but gave up after an angry nine-year-old bit Begw as she attempted to wrestle an ice cream from her.

"Don't get too close to the midgets," said Begw. She popped her head around the door and then headed off to the check-in/check-out counter before the children and their accompanying parents started to arrive.

"Oh, there's a man," said Sketch.

"That's Jake, Fred's dad," said Trevor. "He's the only father here whoever turns up. He stays at home and his wife goes to work in the City." He leaned over and whispered in her ear. "She's a banker."

The surrounding shelves held colourful, well-read books, filled with amazing pictures of children, green aliens and monsters escaped from the imaginations of humans. The children's section also housed books in wooden trains and cars, in which the tiny beings could sit and flick through the pages of their favourites.

From these transport-themed book containers came this week's stories, "The Gruffalo" and "Where The Wild Things Are", both about mythical monsters. Sketch had seen their titles on Amazon but had never read them. She was looking forward to finding out what made them so popular.

"These bundles of germs and bacteria will be all yours next week," said Trevor as a toddler tried to wipe her nose on his trouser leg.

At one thirty, the library was bustling with the sounds of arriving mothers, buggies, bags and tiny children, who all seemed to be trying to escape from their parents.

"Wmduy goo duck," said a little girl with curly hair, pointing towards a nearby bookshelf.

Although Sketch could understand a wide range of languages, she struggled to make out what the small girl and many of the other children were saying, and had no clue what the wailing ones wanted. They made a piercing sound, putting paid to the library rules about people being quiet and talking in whispers. Sketch thought the crying children must have something wrong with them, but their parents seemed unconcerned.

It took twenty minutes for them all to get settled on the floor of the children's library. The mums and Jake held onto their offspring and jiggled them around as Trevor began to read the first story.

As the parents listened and the children fidgeted, Sketch realised she recognised one of them. Where had she seen that young woman? She searched around in her mind, flashing up images of people until it came to her. She hadn't met her, he'd seen her on Facebook. On Matt's Facebook to be precise. It was Ashling, the single mum who was always commenting on his timeline. She looked a little different from her profile picture. Although still pretty, Ashling looked tired, her hair needed washing and her jumper was on backwards. Sketch beamed across to her, forgetting they had not met in real life. She was anxious to talk to this person who knew all about her lovely Matt.

As Trevor finished the session, the mums and Jake began packing up all their belongings, loading up the tots and their sibling babies into buggies. Sketch seized the moment to go and introduce herself to Ashling.

"Hi, Ashling. I'm Sketch." She pushed out her hand toward the other woman.

"Erm, hi. I'm sorry, but how do you know me?" said Ashling.

"Your friends with Matt, aren't you? I'm staying with him. We both love sausages," said Sketch. Her grin spread across her face.

"I used to know him. Sorry, er, Skitch? We've got to go." Ashling dashed off, leaving Sketch open-mouthed.

Trevor approached holding a used tissue by his fingertips.

"Well then, what did you think? Ready to give it a go next week?" he asked.

"Great, fantastic voices for the monsters, "said Sketch. "That girl, Ashling–she seems tired."

"Tired, I should think she's exhausted. She's a single mum, lives on her own. Dropped out of school to take care of the baby. Think she did her exams first."

"Oh. I can't imagine having a child."

"Neither can I. I can hardly feed myself, let alone another human being. So Sketch, you'll do story time next week?"

"Errr, I don't think I'll be good enough," she said. Panic began to rise. Could she cope with another thing to learn?

"Course you will. It's just monsters and snot."

Trevor patted her on the shoulder and headed off to the main area, leaving her to finish clearing up.

Chapter 5

"HELLO, I'M HOME," said Sketch as she came through the red painted front door. Walking through the hall, she caught her reflection in the mirror hanging on the wall and winked at herself. With a job, friends, and a place to live, she felt more like an actual human.

"Hi, Sketch. I'm down in the kitchen. Come and join me for a cuppa. I want to hear all about your first day," said Jackie.

The two women sat around the table drinking chai tea from Jackie's favourite green teapot in mismatched cups. As they drank, Sketch gave Jackie a detailed account of her day, with the exception of her sneaky morning sausage sandwich.

"Sounds to me you've made a good start."

Sketch gave a weak smile.

"You don't seem to happy about it."

"I am," said Sketch. "It's just..."

"What, hon? You can tell me. I promise not to tell anyone."

Sketch bit her lip.

"What if I can't do this? What if I mess up and give someone the wrong books, or can't explain how to use a computer or I can't do voices for the stories like Trevor?"

"You'll be fine," Jackie assured her. She reached over and patted Sketch's hand. "And even if you make a mistake, it won't matter."

"But it will. If I don't learn and show I've changed, I won't be able to go back to the Core."

Jackie walked around the table to where Sketch was sat and put her arms around her.

"I can't pretend to have any idea what it's like in your world but here we help each other and anything I can do to get you home, I will."

Sketch managed a small smile and hugged Jackie back.

"How did you find out about us energies in the Core? Most humans don't know anything about us."

"Now that's a bit of a long one, but it started a couple of years ago. I'd been ill, the flu, and I'd recovered enough to try and catch up with some work. When I tried to log on, I started getting these strange messages. The first one said: We cannot survive without you. I thought perhaps I was hallucinating but I didn't have a fever.

"I carried on, went back to work at the office and forgot all about it, then one night after drinking two or three of glasses of red I got another one: Your assistance is required, Jackie.

"I went to opticians, tried yoga, going to bed at nine o'clock but nothing stopped the messages from popping up on the screen. Part of me wanted to avoid the computer but I needed it to stay in touch with people and for work.

"Then I received a message that said: You have been designated, this is your role. So, then I made an appointment with my GP. I got as far as the surgery waiting room and decided telling the doctor was a bad idea. At best, they would have concerns for my mental health and put me on some horrific drug. Worst case scenario, they section me, and I couldn't end up in hospital. I had Matt to think about."

"What did you do?" asked Sketch, eyes focused on Jackie's lips.

"I decided to reply. The messages were for me, after all." Jackie looked at the time on the kitchen clock.

"God, I'm late for yoga. I'll tell you the rest another time. Will you be alright?"

Sketch nodded.

"The computer's free if you want to use it before Matt gets home from his friend's house."

Sketch took her place in front of the monitor, humming a jingle she'd heard on the telly the night before as she waited for the machine to boot up.

"Inco, it's me Sketch. I know you can hear me and I so wish you were here because the human user world is beyond understanding," she said to the screen. "You can't understand by watching from the Core." She'd not thought about him all day. Instead, her mind had been filled with new and exciting things; stuffed with sausages, stories, Matt, Ashling, Begw, Trevor and the tiny humans. She did want to tell Inco everything she'd seen and heard but she couldn't imagine him there with her. What would his human form look like?

"Inco, I'm going to check out Facebook and Instagram. Begw and Trevor from the library–that's where I work, the library. They said they've sent me friend requests, but you'll have seen them already."

Sketch accepted the friend requests from her two new colleagues and browsed their friends lists to see if there was anyone she could add before turning her attention to Matt's timeline. With no more posts from Ashling, Sketch decided to take matters into her own hands. She pressed the button and sent a friend request into the Facebook ether, with a short personal note attached that read: "Hi Ashling. It's me, Sketch, Matt's friend. I met you at story time today. I'd love to be your friend, too."

Finished on the computer, Sketch curled up on the sofa with a newspaper Jackie picked up on the way home from work. She was still sitting reading when Matt arrived home from his friend's.

"Hiya, Sketch. Did you manage to get a sneaky sausage this morning, then?" he said grinning.

He remembered, Sketch thought. This confirmed they were compatible.

"Yeh, but my boss ate half of it," she said, tilting her head and pushing out her front lip. Matt patted her hair, making her face go red. The blushing was getting to be too much.

"Bad luck," he said. "Plenty more sausages in the freezer." He logged on to the Internet and was gone, off into his own, private zone.

Sketch peered over his shoulders. He was updating his blog. She grabbed her bag from the corner of the kitchen and whipped out her phone. She tapped the touchpad, willing it to connect to the web page she'd bookmarked earlier. Despite the time it took to login to the blog, Matt still hadn't added a new post so Sketch repeatedly refreshed the page until it appeared.

My brain has been invaded, colonized by a girl. Let's call her B. I could describe her to you, but then she might take over your mind too, so I'll keep it brief. B is blonde, tall and gorgeous. She's got a stunning body and she knows it. B is popular, funny and sought after. Then there's me - the complete opposite. I'm a bit geeky, lacking in abs, no money for booze or phones or clothes. I hang out with the comic readers and studious types who don't have girlfriends. But my brain has been invaded and it's imperative I find a way to make B notice me.

I had a plan. One of B's friends is having a party and it's beyond certain that she'll be there. At a party, I could have a couple of drinks, Dutch courage, as they say, and be able to talk to her without stumbling over my words. There might even be a kiss.

Sounds like a great plan, eh? It is, a house party with the adults away celebrating an anniversary is perfect, but there's just one problem. I've not been invited.

"Crap," said Matt out loud. Sketch turned her phone downwards so he couldn't see what she'd been looking at.

"What's wrong?" she asked in a worried tone.

"Nothing you can do anything about. Not unless you've got a copy of the world's best comic going spare."

Sketch's heart sank. She didn't have any comics, let alone one Matt might want. She didn't like to see him sad. It made her feel that way, too. Sketch took this as another sign of their obvious connection and perked up. She would do something to make him happy.

"Why don't you tell me about the comics? I don't own any but we've got some in the library."

Matt laughed.

"The ones in the library are lame. The ones I've got are rare. If I give Dominic a copy of the one he wants I'll never get another one."

"But why would you give it to him if it is so special to you?" asked Sketch looking confused.

"Why, indeed," said Matt. "I want to go to this party, one Rochelle Martin is having, but she's never going to speak to me, let alone ask me to come. Thing is, I know her brother Dominic from comic club. He reckons he can get me in."

"He lives there so he must be able to."

"Exactly, but he'll only agree in return for the third Bird Man comic."

"Oh." Sketch wasn't sure what to say. She didn't want Matt to go to the party either. Not if Britney was going to be there and he planned to kiss her. Her stomach churned and twisted. Why did Matt want Britney when Sketch was right in front of him?

She made her excuses and went up to her room, distraught at what she'd just discovered. She failed to clean her teeth or change her clothes and instead crawled into her bed and pulled the duvet over her head. Sketch found herself unable to cope with the tight feeling in her chest as hot streams of salty water coursed down her cheeks from her eyes, and her nose began to gum up with snot. She laid in bed and cried her first human tears.

Chapter 6

THE LIBRARY WAS busy with older people the next day.

"It's pension day," said Begw. "And the post office is next door. Easy for them to pop in and return their books at the same time they pick up their money." She handed Sketch a pile of novels to place on a trolley. "Plus, there's always someone here who'll speak to them. It's the oldies, the unemployed and parents of small children who keep the remaining libraries open."

Sketch's first Silver Surfers class was at eleven. She went through the training materials and checked that the computers were working.

"Best test them all. These machines are fickle," said Begw.

In addition to routine tests, Sketch asked the energies inside the computers to perform to the best of their ability. *They might not know I'm here but they are my kind*, she thought.

She checked everything three times and highlighted sections of the course materials she might forget. All her efforts went into focusing on the Silver Surfers session. It helped to stop her dwelling upon Matt and his obsession with Britney.

Sketch scanned through the names of the people taking part in her Silver Surfers course over the next six weeks. The six participants included Mr Barrington, who had been wandering around the library for much of the previous day looking confused but content.

"After class, you could get them a *panad* from the drinks machine," said Begw. "Good for bonding," she had said as she gave Sketch money to buy the drinks. "Some of them don't have money for coffee."

Before the session started, the six older people congregated around the computers. They stood behind the chairs as if sitting down might break the machines.

"Hello. I'm Sketch," she said in a voice she hoped was neither too loud for the other book readers in the building nor too quiet for the group and their deteriorated hearing. An induction hearing loop would help people wearing hearing aids to decipher sounds but it was temperamental so she tried to adjust her voice to the right volume.

The group turned, allowing Sketch to see their faces. She recognised Mr Barrington on the right and, to her delight, the lady with the purple, fur-trimmed coat Sketch had seen on her tube journey at the weekend was in the middle of the group.

"I'd like to welcome you all to the Silver Surfers computer training. Can I check who is here?" Sketch checked off their names. In addition to Mr Barrington, there was Flo Foster, Mrs Harding-Edgar, Mr Moore, Annabel Bradford and the lady with the coat was Maud Miller.

"Have any of you ever used a computer before?" Sketch asked smiling at those assembled.

Two hands went up, one belonging to Mr Barrington and the second to Annabel Bradford.

"I've been on the computer at my granddaughter's place. But I couldn't make it work and I was scared of breaking it if I pressed the wrong thing," said Annabel. "My Leanne tried to show me but she went so fast I couldn't keep up."

"Well you've nothing to worry about Annabel," said Sketch. "We're going to start from the very beginning and if something breaks it won't be your fault. We can fix it and anyone can shout if you don't understand something."

She gestured for them to take to their seats and went through some rules the council insists are said every time a course is run, including what to do in the event of a fire. Sketch couldn't imagine this lot stampeding out of the building if the alarm went off, not with all the ladies clutching their bags on their knees and Maud with her trolley squashed next to her chair.

"We're going to do the most important thing first," said Sketch pointing to the power button on the nearest machine. "Switching on the computer." She walked down the line making sure everyone located the button.

"Let's all press together. On the count of three. One, two, three." Sketch held her breath as they switched on their machines. The computers all performed as expected and screens lit up in front of their new users. Sketch said a silent thanks to all her fellow computer energies.

"Brilliant! You can all now switch on a computer. You'll be techies before you know it."

She held up the mouse. "We use this to move around the screen. You can click on the left or on the right, but today we will just be using the left hand side."

The old people held their hands hovered over their mechanical mice.

"Don't expect it to squeak, now. It's not that kind of mouse," Sketch said.

They stared at her, blank expressions on their faces. She thought a joke would help to break the ice, make them less nervous.

"We're going to move our mouse over to the bottom left hand corner of the screen where it says "Start". The little arrow you see is called the cursor," she said. "You have to tell it what to do by moving the mouse."

The Silver Surfers took hold of their mice and tried to make them move as instructed, but instead a comical scene ensued as cursors sped to all corners of the monitor.

"Oh, where's it going?"
"I didn't make it go there."
"How do I get it back?"

Sketch looked on in horror as Flo Foster held her mouse up to her ear and shook it. Why could they not move it properly? How was she going to get them to do to the next task, shutting down and restarting their machine, if they couldn't operate the mouse?

Sketch hadn't anticipated them having physical control problems while using the computer. She wasn't aware it was common for people who'd had no previous knowledge of operating digital devices to find it difficult. She went to each old person, placing her hand on top of theirs, and showing them how to guide the mouse around the screen. It surprised her that their skin felt so different to hers. Their hands showed their age, more than their faces or their physical stature. The skin was wrinkled, cracked and thinning. Through the translucent layer, she could see their veins as blood travelled through them.

Despite Sketch's attempts to get them to handle the mouse in a calm, logical manner, cursors were still running around the screen, like ants on speed. Sketch sighed.

"Don't worry, everyone," she said, though worried herself. "This will get easier the more you practise." No one looked convinced by her words. Sketch stood watching, wondering what to try next when an idea came to her.

On each computer, she downloaded a game from the Library Services Intranet resources page. "Whack-a-Mole" was designed to get the user to hit moles popping up through holes and provided a fun way of practising with the mouse. It took some time before anyone started hitting the rodents with the virtual mallet, but after about five minutes, a voice came from the group.

"I got one!" shouted Maud. The others cheered and then returned to their own games in determined attempts to whack their own moles.

"Well done, Maud," said Sketch giving the enthused woman her best smile. "That's brilliant."

Maud beamed back at her before returning to pursuing virtual moles. At the end of the session they exited the Whack a Mole program, and with some help from Sketch, shut down their computers.

"Thanks so much everyone, you've been amazing. Let's go and get a drink now. They are on me," said Sketch.

The Silver Surfers group colonized one of the larger tables in the social area of the library. A man in his thirties glanced up from his laptop, fished into his pocket and pulled out some yellow foam earplugs. He inserted them into his ears and continued to type.

"So how did you find it?" asked Sketch.

"I thought it was marvelous," said Mrs Harding-Edgar. "I'm a member of all kinds of groups from the Women's Institute to the choir and I meet all these people who want to send photos and invites to things."

"Give it a few sessions and you'll be able to do just that," said Sketch.

"My husband, he was a Colonel in the army, and we went all over the world. Wherever he was stationed, I followed. It was a great life but when we settled in London, everything changed. With all the globetrotting, I'd never had a proper home. You can't imagine how hard is to have no roots. A couple of years ago I decided I'd had enough of sitting in front of the telly, dreaming of the past. So, I started to volunteer at the Community Centre and soon I was doing all sorts of things."

"Oh, it's hard," said Maud. "I've lived here all my life, but people move on. They die or you stop seeing them. I'm pleased I've got my cat, Clock, for company. You're never alone with a pet."

"Isn't Clock a rather unusual name for a cat?" asked Sketch taking a sip of her hot chocolate and savouring its warm sweetness.

Maud chuckled. "My grandson Martin chose her when he was small. He's much older now and lives with his parents in Australia. Sydney, that's where they stay. Not seen them for three years, but then they're happy."

Sketch thought Maud's smile didn't quite reach her eyes, contradicting her positive words. She understood how it felt to be far away from everything familiar.

"How often do you speak to them?" asked Annabel Bradford, perfectly dressed in a winter woolen suit. "It's expensive to call overseas and even more on a portable phone."

"Oh, it's not as much as it was," replied Maud. "We muddle by. The best news is they've promised to buy me a computer so we can chat on something called Skype. I'll be able to see their faces. Can you imagine that?"

"Doesn't seem five minutes since we were all on rations and now we can talk to people on the other side of the world." Annabel shook her head.

"That's why I'm here. I'm awful terrified I'm going to break it, so when I saw the poster about this course, it seemed angel-sent," said Maud.

Sketch patted Maud on the hand. "You'll be Skyping away to Australia in no time Maud." She hoped she could help Maud. And not because it was her way back to the Core but because she liked her.

"Okay everyone, I have to get back to work, but well done again. I'll see you all for class next week but remember you can book in to use the computers here and practise your new skills."

The older people got their belongings together and said goodbye as Sketch tidied up the disposable cups from the table, smiling to herself.

"You seem happier," said Begw as she walked past with a trolley of books to be shelved. "You looked well fed up this morning."

"I was sad about a boy, but my class was brilliant. I loved it."

"Oh. Cool," said Begw. "Boys are smelly. You don't want to be bothering with them. Get yourself off with Trevor for lunch, tell him all about it. He loves a good drama."

The sun shone warming the air and putting smiles on the faces of Londoners as Trevor and Sketch took to the streets to eat their lunch. They swapped sandwiches and shared a can of cola from a shop near the library.

"What's this about you having problems with your Matt?" asked Trevor. "Want to tell me about it? I might be able to help."

Sketch nodded, her mouth full of carrot and hummus on whole meal bread. After quickly chewing and swallowing the sandwich, she began to tell Trevor about Matt.

"He's not really *my* Matt. I just want him to be. The thing is, he goes on and on about a girl named Britney from his college, and I thought, because we both like sausages, it must mean something." She swept the remaining crumbs from her jacket and looked up at Trevor.

"I feel stupid but I can't stop liking him," she sighed. "What can I do?"

"If you want my advice," said Trevor dodging some school kids coming toward them in a large, noisy gaggle. "This Britney doesn't sound very interested in Matt, so let him keep trying. Eventually, she'll let him down and then you'll get your chance to make him see how wonderful and gorgeous you are."

Sketch thought about this. Trevor's advice made sense and lifted some of the fog of misery that descended when she thought about Matt.

"Isn't there a quicker way?" she asked.

"You can try but whilst he's got his mind set on her, you'll not get too far."

Whilst not perfect, the idea of playing the long game gave Sketch something practical to focus on. In the meantime, she would concentrate on becoming his friend and getting him an invite for the party without him parting ways with his prized Birdman comic.

Chapter 7

JACKIE SAT in front of the computer. It had been pulled away from the wall and its cables and sockets were on view.

"Is everything alright?" asked Sketch putting down her bag and peering over at her host.

"I'm not sure. I not an expert with machines but the device they gave me to communicate with your world isn't connecting."

"Oh, you have a device?"

"They gave it to me so I could be contacted and I'm supposed to report on you, tell them how you're getting on with it."

"Why don't you show me what you did and I'll see if I can help," Sketch told Jackie. Things appeared different from the outside, but her knowledge of computers still exceeded Jackie's.

Jackie took out the device and inserted it into a USB port. A flashing cursor appeared on the screen.

"What now?" asked Sketch.

Jackie began to type.

Liaison Human User Jackie checking in.

The cursor blinked as they waited for a response but nothing happened.

Liaison Human User Jackie checking in for update purposes.

She pressed enter and waited.

"Why is nothing happening?"

"I'm not sure," said Sketch. "Have you tried switching the computer on and off?"

Jackie scowled at her. "Even *I* know to do that. It's like computer for dummies."

"Sorry. It does work in ninety percent of cases," said Sketch.

"I know. Sorry for snapping. I'm not very good with these things."

"Give it another go."

Jackie pressed enter repeatedly but nothing happened. Sketch fiddled around with cables and settings on the computer but it made no difference.

"Something must be wrong with the device," said Sketch. "Don't look so worried, Jackie. I'm sure they're aware of it and will sort something out."

"I just wanted to let the One know how well you've been doing in your first week here."

Sketch beamed. "Really?"

"Yes, of course. You fit right in. Now let's not worry about this for while," the other woman said, ejecting the USB device and zipping it into a pocket of her handbag. "Tell me about your first IT class."

Jackie set about preparing for dinner, stew warming at a low temperature on the hob as she listened to Sketch.

"Do you think it means something that Maud, the old lady from the Tube, turned up at my class today?"

"Probably not. There's a lot of people living in London but it can still be a small place."

"It must be lonely living on your own," said Sketch. "I've never been on my own." She thought about the energies that surrounded her in the Core. To be without others wasn't a concept which was understood by them.

"Some people like it. If you're used to being around others, it can be lonely, especially if you don't have any other choice."

"Maybe we should do something. Shall I invite her for tea?" asked Sketch.

"Nice idea but best to wait until you've got to know her a bit better."

Sketch nodded. "Ok, I'm going up to my room for a while."

"Tea's in about half an hour. I'll give you a shout when it's ready."

Sketch headed up the stairs thinking about the oddness of the English language. Tea could be a drink and also the name of a meal. She didn't know how, but it was somehow possible to know which thing someone was talking about. Human brains must be complex to understand the difference.

She settled herself down on her bed, cross-legged and took out her phone from her pocket. A series of alerts pinged her screen, one of which was an event invitation. Accessing the app, Sketch read the details. It came from Begw, inviting her to drinks after work on Friday at The Junction Tavern, a local pub. Trevor was invited, too.

Sketch fizzled inside, resisting the urge to jump up and down on her mattress. She accepted the invite and switched to see if Ashling had responded to her friend request. She had not.

Perhaps she's not had a chance to look at her Facebook or she doesn't recognise me from my profile photo, she thought.

Begw's invitation to the pub gave her an idea. If she made friends with someone going to Rochelle's party, maybe she would able to get both Matt and herself an invite. Dominic, Rochelle's brother was an obvious choice.

She thought about how people make friends with others. Quite often they had something in common but, like Matt, Sketch had no comics to trade with him. She searched for him on Facebook and found him within a few minutes on Matt's list of people he went to college with. She sent her friend request without an accompanying message, hoping he would either think she was someone he'd met or be intrigued enough to click accept.

Five minutes later her phone pinged again, notifying her of a new virtual friend. *It's going to be either Dominic or Ashling*, she thought, unclear in her mind as to which she'd prefer. A glance at the screen confirmed it was Dominic. She posted a comment on his timeline.

Thanks for the add, she'd written.

Hopefully, this would start off a conversation.

"Sketch," Jackie called. "Tea's ready."

She checked her phone again but decided to leave it in her room. Jackie frowned upon anyone looking at them during mealtimes, and if Dominic did reply, it would do him no harm to wait.

Sketch noticed Matt didn't talk much to his mum about Britney, so she was careful not to ask him any sensitive questions at the table. She needed to know more about Britney, the party, Dominic and graphic novels. Then she could be more supportive, like a proper friend. She chose to start with the latter.

"Matt, could I borrow one of your comics? I've never read one and they sound fun."

Matt raised his eyebrows and his face displayed a semblance of a smile.

"Yeh, I'll get you some from my room after dinner. Just don't, whatever you do, spill anything on them, or take them out of the house."

"He's dead fussy about them. Got a list of rules longer than your arm…longer than anyone's arm, in fact," said Jackie.

"They're valuable, Mum. You don't understand," said Matt directing a frown at his mother.

Brilliant, thought Sketch. This was part one of her plan. Tonight she'd learn everything she could about comics, read them, Google them, and ask Matt questions. And tomorrow, she'd follow up with Dominic. She felt proud of herself. She was learning how to help humans, just as instructed by the One.

Before going to bed, a flashing notification on her phone caught her eye. Dominic had replied.

Hi Sketch. Nice hair. ;-)

You think so? she wrote back.

I do. Suits you. What you up to?

Remembering her plan, she resisted being drawn into a series of messages and replied that she was off to sleep before saying goodnight and turning off her phone.

Over the following days, Sketch and Dominic became acquainted by the magic of the Internet, distracting her from Matt and the periodic homesickness, which hit her when thinking of Inco. She stopped talking to him through the screen, telling herself he could observe everything going on in her life without a verbal breakdown.

Thursday evening, after an hour long session about the virtues of comics and a discussion of their favourite Marvel superheroes, they reached the subject of the party.

Sketch, you're in London, right?

Yeh, I shouldn't say where, in case you're a dodgy old man.

*Moi? *Shocked, sad face**

Shut up!

You're right. Anyway, my sister is throwing a house party next Saturday and it's…it's stupid. Don't worry.

Tell me.

Well, do you want to come?

Sketch thought about it. This is what she'd been working towards but although meeting Dominic sounded exciting, she couldn't go without Matt.

I'd love to come but I've got a friend staying with me for the weekend. Can I bring them, too? Would you mind?

The screen of her phone remained blank. Minutes passed without a response from Dominic. She paced around her room, checking her phone settings in case the Wi-Fi signal had disconnected. Time slowed to a pattern where seconds felt like hours. Of course he wouldn't want her to bring a friend. It was obvious even to Sketch that Dominic had a crush on her. She turned off the volume on her mobile, picked up a comic and attempted to distract herself from the waiting.

Five minutes went by before she turned over her phone and, at last, there was a message from Dominic. Her heart thumped and she stared at the notification. What if he said no? What would she do then? The phone kept blinking at her, insisting she read his reply.

She pressed the screen and the message popped onto the screen. Efficient energies lived inside it.

Soz, my Mum called me. No worries – bring your friend. Invite as many people as you like.

Sketch took a gulp of air and let out a breath in relief. The plan was going to work. She never had anything to worry about.

She skidded along the corridor to Matt's room and pounded on his door.

"Yurgahey." Matt's head emerged from around the door. "Sleep," he said in explanation.

"I've got us an invite to the party. We're official." Sketch held up her hand for a high-five but Matt ignored it, picking her up and spinning her around before enclosing her in a giant hug. She smelt his body through his crumpled t-shirt and felt its heat as he squeezed her. She closed her eyes trying to capture all the details of the moment.

Matt pulled away.

"How did you do it? Who's invited us?"

"Dominic," said Sketch grinning.

"How do you know Dom? Why's he letting me come, too?"

"I added him on Facebook. We've been messaging. I think he's kind of funny. I just talked to him a lot about the comics you lent me and he seemed to like me."

"Sketch, you are too clever."

"One thing. He told me I can bring who I like but I didn't tell him it was you. Didn't want him to get all funny about the Birdman comic," she said.

"Don't worry. I'll not mention it to him. If he asks I'll tell him I've changed my mind and once I'm at the party with you, it won't matter."

Chapter 8

ON FRIDAY, the end of Sketch's first week working at the library, Maud came in to practise her IT skills. Sketch watched as the older lady loaded up the computer and gave her a hand to open Whack-A-Mole. Whilst the machine whizzed and whirred and its energies did their technological magic, the pair chatted.

"The week's been quiet, Sketch. I've seen plenty of that daytime telly but it's not up to much," she smiled. "A lot of shouting and picking faults with people, so I thought I'd come down here and have a go at hitting some mice."

Sketch giggled at Maud's mixed up words. She thought the lady winked at her but Sketch couldn't decide whether she imagined it or not.

"Well, we're glad you're here. Just give me a shout if you want a hand with anything."

Sketch kept an eye on Maud from across the shelves of books as she stacked, pleased to see how well she was coming along with the mouse control exercise. Mr Barrington also dropped by but by the time he'd reached the counter to book a computer, he'd forgotten why he was there. Sketch thought he might be lonely, too, like Maud. He spent a lot of time in the library, so either he loved it there or it wasn't so much fun for him at home. Sketch liked the library and could see its appeal, but suspected the latter was the real reason. The library gave Mr Barrington, with his short-term memory problems, a safe space to be.

"Sketch," said Maud waving from across the library. "I've finished now. I'm going for a cuppa at the café across the road. Do you want to come, too?"

"Oh, I'd love to Maud but I've got books to put back on the shelves. Another time, maybe?"

Maud nodded. "Alright, love. That'd be nice."

Maud looked disappointed. Sketch wished she could join her. Maud seemed to be reaching out for some company.

"Begw?"

Sketch's boss turned around, flicking her fringe out of the way.

"Yeh?"

"Can we switch our lunches, please? It's really important. Please," she said.

Begw wrinkled her nose, assuming a near frown.

"Oh, go on then. I heard you talking to that old lady. It's a nice thing to do. Don't be late back."

"Thank you."

"Don't look so surprised. We North Walians are super nice."

Sketch dashed off after Maud and found her about to sit down in the café.

"Can I have a decaf skinny gingerbread latte please?" Sketch asked the barista behind the counter as she waved to Maud. The old lady's face lit up when she saw the blonde-haired woman entering the café.

"Begw let me off early," she explained.

"That's good. I just wanted a way to say thank you for being kind to me at class last week."

Maud insisted on paying for the drink her friend had ordered herself.

"It's amazing all the variations of coffee and tea you can choose these days. I'm a simple tea with milk and a sugar girl."

"There's no need to thank me or buy me coffee. It's my job, Maud. And you are getting on so well with the computer now."

Maud patted her hand.

"Och, it's kind of you to say that but learning new things is not so easy for us old fuddy-duddies. It's just so important to me to be able to use the computer."

The old lady pulled a purse from her bag, opening it to show a picture of a sandy-haired man and a lady, both in their mid-forties. In front of them was a teenage boy sporting a cheeky grin, ginger hair, and a face full of freckles.

"This is my family in Australia. I miss them so terribly you see. Can't tell them, though, can I?"

"My family is a long way away too, or it seems like it, anyway," said Sketch. "Sometimes I close my eyes, block out all the noise, and pretend they're next to me."

"Well, I'm sure they're missing you and I bet you've plenty of friends here," smile Maud.

Sketch nodded. "I've met a few people."

Maud chatted about her grandson and her family in the southern hemisphere.

"I'm so proud of Martin. He's the star of his school's cricket team, you know."

Sketch thought of Inco for the first time since the beginning of the week. She missed the bond they shared. They were in many ways the same; he was the closest thing to a human family she had. She reminded herself to give him an update via the computer after she got in from the pub.

"Maud?" asked Sketch. "What happened to your husband? Did he, er…pass on?"

"No, Sketch. He didn't die. He ran off with a woman ten years younger than me. Such a cliché. He was the Bank Manager and he took up with his assistant."

"Oh, I'm so sorry. That's even worse. Or maybe it's not. Sorry."

Sketch decided to stop talking before any other idiotic things escaped from her mouth

"Oh, no. There's nothing at all to apologise for. It was over forty years ago when my son was just a little boy," Maud smiled. "So, do you have a young man, then, Sketch? Someone you're sweet on?"

People kept asking her this and she didn't know how to answer except with a version of the truth.

"I like this boy named Matt but he likes this girl who doesn't like him," she said. Talking about it made her stomach churn and her eyes get watery.

"Now it's my turn to say sorry. But if this Matt can't see how special you are he isn't worth the bother. A pretty thing like you will soon find someone else. You won't believe me now but that's the truth. Best to learn it when you're young rather than ending up one of those women who end up with someone who's not good enough for them."

Sketch didn't know what to say. She looked up at the clock.

"I'm afraid I've got to go back to work now Maud, so Begw can go to lunch. Maybe we can do this again sometime. At the weekend, perhaps?" asked Sketch.

"I would enjoy that."

Sketch's afternoon passed by in a blur of book, CD, DVD and newspaper filing. Newspapers were a source of interest for Sketch, informing her about life in the world outside of her small bit of North London. Energies in the Core absorbed news of the outer world via the web browser, on the BBC pages where Jackie read the latest bulletins, with the occasional visit to The Guardian and Al Jazeera's webpages. The newspapers, in comparison, with their differing perspectives were both refreshing and confusing. Some of them Sketch found difficult to believe.

If you took everything you read in them to be factual, you would never leave the house, she thought. The world, according to the media, was bleak one.

At the end of the day, the three library workers shut down the computers, turned off the lights, and locked the doors in readiness for the staff excursion to the pub.

"I'm dying for a pint," said Begw, zipping up her coat as she stepped out into the cold November night air.

"Me too," said Trevor. "What's your tipple, Sketch?"

Sketch stared blankly at Trevor. This was one of those examples of colloquial language that fell out of the scope of her data download.

"What drink do you prefer? Cider? Lager? Spirits? Or are you more of an alcopops girl?"

"Err, I don't drink that much," said Sketch aware she'd never had any alcohol before. She worried about the power of the strange toxic liquids. People posted disturbing photos on the Internet and made claims of being sick as a result of drinking too much alcohol. Sketch hoped there was more to having a pint than just ending up with her head stuck down a toilet. Getting so drunk she couldn't walk straight wouldn't be a good impression to give her boss and she couldn't risk the news reaching the One; she might never be allowed to return to the computer again. The outside world wasn't as scary as she'd imagined but it wasn't her world. The thoughts triggered a pang of longing for the world of circuits, operating systems and programs so familiar to her.

"Oh," said Begw. "You're underage." She looked at Trevor. He shrugged.

"What does that mean?" asked Sketch.

"Alcohol in the pub's just for adults. Eighteen or over, you have to be."

Sketch's smile vanished.

"But it's sixteen if you're having a meal," said Trevor.

"Ah, so it is," said Begw. "Mind you, I shouldn't be encouraging underage binge drinking."

"Begw Jones, are you telling me you didn't drink in the pub before your eighteenth birthday," said Trevor.

"You're right," she turned to Sketch who was still not sure if not drinking was a good thing or not. "We could order a meal. You fancy a burger, Sketch?"

Sketch spent most of the seven-minute walk to the pub thinking about what she should drink and by the time they had reached the Junction Taverns she'd made up her mind.

"I'll have a pint of cider, please," she said, resolving to sip it. This would be excellent preparation for next week's party.

The Junction Tavern was a gastropub, a concept invented by the hospitality industry to convince non-drinkers to visit pubs more often. They served food a notch up from chicken in a basket but not so posh it came with smears on plates.

"The food's alright here, a bit pricey," said Begw.

"It is on the wages the council pays," said Trevor. "Better to spend them sinking a few after work."

"It's busy in here," said Sketch. The pub was the most crowded place she'd been in.

"Full of people who stagger onto the underground buses and trains at the end of night," said Trevor. "Commuters."

Begw had reserved a small table for the three of them, as she didn't want to end up in the garden area with what she called "the dirty smokers". Sketch found the smell of cigarette smoke repulsive.

"Why do people enjoy putting something in their mouth they've set fire to? Aren't they scared of getting burnt?"

Begw laughed and Trevor snorted out some of his beer through his nose.

"You're a funny one, Sketch, but well done for your first week. Be sure and come back on Monday," said Begw.

One of the barmen came around lighting candles on each of the tables. Sketch edged her chair back from the naked flame, and took her first sip of alcohol. She swilled it around her mouth, exploring the liquid with her tongue. It was foul. She struggled not to spit it out, not wanting to appear ungrateful.

"So, Sketch, how have you found your first week?" asked Trevor.

"It's been brilliant. I'm learning so much from you both, and even from the old people in my Silver Surfers group."

Both Begw and Trevor looked at each other across the table and laughed.

"Try working there for three years and you'll find it's not as great as it seems," said Begw taking gulps of her cider.

"You don't like it then?" asked Sketch.

"It's not that I don't like it. It's just that Winston, the area boss from the council, is such a cock."

Sketch hadn't met Winston but even *she* knew he wasn't going to be a giant penis in real life. Her brain was beginning to understand language better and she realised Begw meant Winston was not a likeable man.

"He runs around slashing budgets and trying to see down my top. He doesn't care whether the library is here or not."

"It's a massive battle we're fighting," added Trevor.

"Fightin'," said Begw, accentuating her Welsh accent.

"Fightin'," said Trevor. "There's a rumour going round they'll try and shut us down."

"Over my dead body," said Begw.

Sketch continued to sip at her cider. It was going down much quicker than she'd expected.

"Where do you think all those mums and tots and handsome Jake would go if we weren't there with story time?" Trevor began to rant.

The mention of story time reminded Sketch of Ashling. She'd heard nothing from her on Facebook.

"Do you know the girl with the long blond hair and the little boy at story time on Monday?" she said looking between Trevor and Begw.

"Yeh, Ashling? She lives down the road from me," said Begw. "See her out with the sprog sometimes."

"Does she live with her mum and dad?"

"No, she lives on her own – had been in a hostel, I think, but now she's got a council flat. Why do you ask?"

Sketch wasn't sure how best to answer Begw's question. She couldn't say, "Because she knows the boy I love and I want to get to be her friend so she can tell me more about him."

"I dunno. She just looked a bit sad and lonely."

"She probably is. There's a lot of sad and lonely around in this city," said Trevor. "And lots of them are single mums and the occasional single dad."

"Enough," declared Begw looking up from her iPhone. "Enough work talk, let's get down to some serious drinking."

By the time they all left the pub three hours later Sketch was suffering the effects of too much cider. Despite it being just half past eight, she felt as if she should have been in her bed hours before. Bed and sausages were the only two things she could think of.

"I need a saussaage," she slurred. She looked around but all the weekday sausage-selling fast food outlets had closed for the day.

"Ohhhh,"said Trevor. "Don't we all."

Begw rolled her eyes and steadied Sketch, who was losing her battle with gravity.

"You'll only get a kebab at this time of night."

"No, I want a sausssage," said Sketch.

"Trust me. What you need is a kebab," said Begw who was experienced at both being drunk and dealing with the intoxicated.

They pointed Sketch toward Tufnell Park Kebabs before they headed off in two different directions to meet friends.

The colours on the menu board went blurry around her and she slurred her words as she ordered a sausage. The people behind the counter in the kebab shop were more than proficient at translating drunk into whole sentences and provided Sketch with a kebab and a matching portion of greasy chips.

Chapter 9

IN THE EARLY hours of Saturday morning, Sketch rediscovered the remains of her drunken food binge. She awoke still wearing the previous day's clothing with bits of cold, squashed chips attached to the side of her face and congealed tomato ketchup stains on her t-shirt. With one hand, she reached up to touch her head, wondering where the incessant pain was coming from and with the other groped around on the floor beside her bed for the bottle of cola she thought she had bought the night before, but failed to find it. The stabbing sensation in her head lessened when she moved it to a cooler spot on the pillow, angling it in a certain direction, but the relief didn't last for long. Sketch's attention skipped between the drilling sensation in her head and the swirling, sick feeling rising up from her stomach, up through her body in violent waves, which threatened to rush from her mouth. Anxious not to add to the drunken carnage she'd created in the room she ran, hand covering her lips to the bathroom and positioned herself over the toilet bowl.

Why did I do this? she thought. *Why did I keep drinking?*

She scanned through her memories of the evening but they were patchy, a flash of a funny moment there, the sensation of feeling part of something and a memory she'd enjoyed it all but the specifics remained vague. Her mind leapt as she remembered Trevor taking photos on his phone. What if he's posted them on Facebook or Instagram? All her new friends would see them and… and everyone in the Core.

Sketch lay down on the bathroom floor, its cool tiles providing some relief from the pain. She drifted between surges of nausea and sleep, jolting back to alertness by a frantic knocking on the door.

"Sketch? Are you ok?" said Jackie.

"Never, ever again will I drink beer, or wine or cider," she said shuffling into the corridor.

Jackie laughed. "I've heard that before. You do look a bit green, Sketch," she said, locking herself into the toilet.

"I'm so sorry, Jackie. Please don't say anything to it about this?"

"Say anything to who?"

"The One," said Sketch in a whisper.

"Who?" shouted Jackie through the wooden door.

"The One. I won't be allowed to go back."

Sketch sank down onto the corridor floor, her back against the peach-coloured wall, and began to sob.

The toilet flushed and the sound of running water seemed to synchronise with the tears cascading down her face.

"I'm stuck in an alien world. I don't belong here and I'm scared I'll never be able to go back."

"It's alright." Jackie sat down on the floor next to her guest and put her arm around her. "You're not the first person to have drunk too much and you won't be the last."

"It's not that. I…I miss Inco. I miss not having a body." A large single tear fell silently down her face.

"It's perfectly normal for you to feel homesick," said Jackie putting her arms around Sketch.

"It hurts. It hurts like my head or my tummy but I can't find where it comes from. I need to make it stop."

"It will, don't worry, it will. Everything will be okay. I can't imagine how I'd feel in your position, if you put me inside a computer, but it's not for long."

"They won't let me come back if they find out about this." Sketch hung her head and gazed at the carpet.

"Now you're to stop thinking like that," said Jackie, her tone firmer and more parent-like. Sketch nodded and sniffed. "I'll get you some tissue for your nose."

Sketch still thought Jackie didn't understand her. How could she? How could anyone comprehend what it was like to fail at everything?

Her thoughts halted as she bolted for the bathroom. "I'm going to be sick."

Despite Jackie administering a bacon sandwich, Alka Seltzer, and an inordinate quantity of tea, a hangover cure she claimed never failed to work for her, Sketch crawled back into bed, feeling sorry for herself. She emerged in the evening, able to eat but still unable to think about alcohol without experiencing a physical reaction in her gut.

"You any better, hon?" asked Jackie, looking up from her TV programme, smiling at Sketch.

Sketch nodded. "Thank you Jackie. You've been so kind but…"

"But what?"

Sketch took a deep breath as if the extra air would give her confidence. "I don't think it's working here. I want to go back to the Core, to the computer. They might recycle me; I might become a stone or piece of plastic but then at least I won't harm anyone or anything."

"Oh Sketch, you've had a rough day. I understand why you'd want to leave but you can't right now."

"Why not? I'm no use to anyone here," said Sketch, her whole face frowning and her fists clenched into tight balls of bone, skin and muscle. "I need to go."

"Now, that's not true. You've been helping people in the library and Matt says you're going to a party with him next week. He even smiled and that doesn't happen very often, believe me. "

"Matt can't go on his own," said Sketch under her breath. Jackie edged closer to her. "He has to come with me."

"And what about that old lady you've adopted, Maisie?"

"It's Maud," said Sketch remembering her promise to meet her for coffee tomorrow. "Someone else can teach them all IT, someone better than me." She hated having a body, being tied to the humans, and still messing everything up.

"Look, Sketch, you're sad and tired, which isn't the best time to make important decisions," said Jackie. "I think you need to get some more rest. Grab a cushion and a blanket, and sit on the sofa with me. There's something I think you should watch." Jackie selected a DVD from a small pile on the bookcase and the pair settled down to watch *It's A Wonderful Life*.

The film distracted Sketch. She found the black and white cinematography soothing, as it showed world closer in its resemblance to the monochrome of the Core than contemporary London.

"What did you think, then?" asked Jackie as the credits began to scroll down the screen.

"I guess George Bailey felt like me."

"Yes, and he had no idea how important he was to others, just like you."

"Does that make you my guardian angel?" asked Sketch, a grin taking root on her face.

"I suppose it does."

Sketch arrived at the café ahead of time. She watched as Maud, handbag hanging over the arm of her purple coat, picked her way along the street with the aid of a wooden stick. When she talked to Maud and most of the other members of the group there seemed no difference in their ages, but physically she could see their bodies had decayed. How must it be for your structure to fail you?

The pair ordered mugs of tea and iced cakes Maud called buns.

"Maud," she said. "Are you afraid of me?"

"No, of course not. What a funny question."

"I'm sorry. Did I offend you?"

Maud shook her head. "I wouldn't be here drinking tea if I didn't like you."

Sketch smiled. She took out a list compiled in her room the night before, of questions she wanted to ask, things to help her succeed in understanding humans better.

"I read that people who are old don't like teenagers. A newspaper article said they're scared of them, especially the ones with hoods on their jumpers."

"You'd best not believe everything you read in the paper," said Maud, wiping the condensation made by her tea from her glasses. "We don't often meet people of your generation and it's easy for some to believe everything they see on the news."

Sketch listened as Maud explained about the riots that had taken place in the summer.

"Why would people do that? Set fire to things and steal from shops? You must have been terrified."

"No shop on my street, so it was safe. And it wasn't *all* young people of course, but to watch the news you'd think it was."

Maud's words filtered through Sketch's mind. Older people saw teenagers in groups hanging outside stores, in dark streets and bus stops. They looked intimidating to them because of stereotyping by the media, and because they walked along pavements in groups, their loud voices dominating.

"It's a shame," said Sketch. "All the older people I've met are lovely, and you know so many things about the world." As she spoke, an idea formed in her mind.

"What's making you smile like that?" asked Maud.

"Just a little plan I've got." Sketch leant over the table. "Can I share it with you?"

That evening Sketch secured the computer to herself for half an hour before Jackie got home from picking up Matt from his dad's house in Beckenham.

"Hi, Inco. Are you there? I hope so. I'm sorry I've not been around but I feel the absence of you, of the Core. This world is not as simple as I thought. The humans are complex and I'm finding new ways to learn about them." She paused before going on. "Yesterday, I was sick. The worst thing is knowing that I've done it to myself, like a kind of self-sabotage. But making mistakes can be a good thing. How else would I know how much to drink or not drink? Or how humans feel when people they love don't love them back?"

"Next week I'm going to a party with Matt. It's so I can be there when Britney rejects him and then he might see me and want to kiss me instead."

She outlined the plan she'd made with Maud, hoping it would impress them all and shut down the computer as requested by Jackie. There was still no sign of Ashling online but it was story time the next day at the library, so Sketch would have a chance to speak to her then.

Chapter 10

WITH SO MANY books in the children's section of the library, Sketch struggled to decide which to choose to read to her tiny audience. There were fabulous tales of monsters, families, bogies, fairies and being scared in the dark. The engaging words of books danced with tantalising illustrations in vibrant colours.

Children are luckier than adults, thought Sketch.

Adult books are filled with words, thousands of them but no one thought to add pictures to their stories, unless you counted comics. And their readership was in the minority, if library borrowing figures were accurate. With less than an hour until the tots arrived, Sketch turned to Trevor for help selecting the right books for their age group.

"Children are similar to caterpillars – I suppose they're a bit more attractive," he said handing her a well-thumbed large-sized copy of *The Very Hungry Caterpillar*. "They both eat and eat and eat, and when they've finished eating they have a sleep. After some time, they blossom into amazing and diverse creatures after their awkward teenage cocoon period. However, some of them turn into Daily Mail readers–the children that is, not the caterpillars."

To accompany the Eric Carle classic, he chose *Giraffes Can't*

Dance, knowing all the children loved it and like to pretend to be the animals. "Let 'em wriggle around a bit. You can too if you fancy."

"I'm a bit nervous," said Sketch leafing through the book.

"You'll do great. Them oldies love you, so why wouldn't the kids? I'll be around. If you need me just wave."

As with the previous week, parents began bringing their children into the library well before the storytelling session was due to start. They arrived with sniffles, voices and howls. Winter temperatures meant they were wrapped up in giant padded coats, baby grow ski suits, gloves, hats and scarves. One by one, parents peeled off their children's layers and staked their place on the library floor. With them all camped out and ready Sketch, entered the room. She smiled at them, scanning the expectant faces for Ashling and her little boy, but they were not there. Maybe they were running late.

"Hello, everyone. I'm Sketch. I think I met most of you last week. Trevor thought it would be a nice change for you to have a different storyteller for a few weeks," she said. "It's my first time so sorry if it's not very good."

"Oh, I'm sure you'll be just fine," said Jake juggling his little one on his knee. "It'll be interesting to have a different voice."

"I love children's books," said Sketch.

"I think we all do. Sometimes I think we enjoy them more than the children," said one of the mums with a chuckle.

Sketch glanced up at the digital clock hung on the wall above the bookcases. It didn't look like Ashling was coming and she couldn't delay the start of the session any further.

"Most of you regulars are here so we'll get going and anyone who arrives late can just join in."

Delving into the first story distracted Sketch from thoughts of Ashling, Matt or her fear of not being able to return to the Core. She took on the personas of the characters and the voice of the narrator and even the most fidgety of children in the group sat still, at least for part of the hour.

With Sketch on a high from the success of story time, she forgot about the non-appearance of Ashling. As the week progressed she was kept busy with the Silver Surfers. They gained confidence and became easier to teach, having mastered mouse control. Requests to play Whack-A-Mole increased so much that Sketch made a note to herself not to introduce them to more addictive games like Candy Crush Saga. With some basics in place, they moved onto setting up email accounts and sending their first email.

"Whoop!" said Mr Barrington as a ping indicated the arrival of an email from Maud. "It's so fast. Imagine if we'd had this during the war. We would've beaten those Germans." Everyone laughed.

"I've no idea what I was so scared of," said Flo. "We'll all be scanning the World Inter Web next."

It wasn't until Thursday evening when Jackie recounted her day, that Sketch remembered Ashling. Jackie's firm hosted an away day at a hotel on the outskirts of London with the aim of bonding people in the department.

"I'm not sure anyone bonded but my team, the green team. We won a mug," she said proudly, placing the ceramic cup on the table.

"It's…" Sketch began, not knowing how to describe the mug without dampening Jackie's excitement. It looked like an ordinary supermarket cup to her. Not pretty or special, just a mug.

"Oh, I know it's nothing to look at, but my team won it," said Jackie gazing at the prize.

"For what?" asked Sketch, confused as to what they'd possibly have to do to win it.

"Well, first we had fifteen minutes to make a bridge out of newspaper. It had to hold an apple without it falling down. Just paper. Nothing else."

Sketch nodded but still didn't understand why Jackie was so excited.

"We aced it! We worked so well together. There were other tests, too, and overall, we won."

Maybe it's just the winning that was important, thought Sketch.

"Debs, she's on the green team too, she's going to give her mug to Patsy, her daughter who's eight. Isn't that sweet? Debs is a single mum and she is brilliant with Patsy. She loves her so much."

It was Jackie's mention of lone parenting that reminded Sketch of Ashling. She'd not been on any social media all week. Sketch wondered if something had happened to her.

The thought burrowed into her mind, keeping her awake at night as she struggled to sleep. She pulled out a notebook from the side of her bed and wrote down her worries.

1. Ashling is sick and stuck in her flat.
2. Sammy is sick.
3. Sammy's dad has come back and they have gone to live with him.
4. Both Ashling and Sammy are sick.
5. They're being held hostage in Ashling's flat by a crazed burglar.

Putting her thoughts down on paper didn't help to still her mind, so after a failed attempt at counting sheep, she gave up and went downstairs to watch TV. With nothing of interest to watch in the middle of the night, Sketch snuggled down on the sofa and, still thinking about Ashling, fell asleep.

The next day, Sketch woke without any energy. Used to being the one who made things happen, shifting them at will around a screen, she was uncomfortable with the idea that it now seemed a mammoth task to put one size six foot in front of the other. The heaviness and lethargy of her body appeared alongside an apparent inability to be positive or speak in sentences that made sense. Her disengaged mood didn't escape the attention of her colleagues at the library.

"You look like you need a sausage sarnie," said Begw. "You can go and get one if you like." Sketch looked back at her and grimaced, suspecting Begw planned to steal it.

"You're not the only one having a bad day," said Begw. "I've been at a libraries division meeting this morning with Winston."

"Bad then?" asked Trevor.

"You don't want to know," said Begw, shaking her head. "Are you sure you're alright, Sketch? You look like someone stole all your computers."

"No sleep," replied Sketch.

"Ah, that would do it. Thought you'd been out on the booze again."

Begw handed her a strong cup of black coffee. "Here this should keep you awake. Why don't you stay in the back this morning? There's a pile of new batch books just come in for cataloguing."

Cataloguing books was easy. It entailed entering all the details to the computer, generating a bar code and sticking it on the inside cover of the book. Then you placed the novel or work of non-fiction into a plastic jacket containing a security job. Even Sketch doubted she would mess it up. She was relieved not to have to speak to the public and she could have as much tea and coffee as she liked.

Midway through the morning she pressed a wrong key and pulled up a list of library members, containing all the information provided by people when they registered. It included their names, date of birth, email and physical address. She understood the data was confidential but it wouldn't do any harm to have a peek at where Ashling lived. If she'd fallen down the stairs, there would be no one to ring for an ambulance or look after her little boy.

The terrible scenarios conjured by her mind gave her the courage to type Ashling's name into the computer program. Up popped an address of a council estate in Brecknock Road. Sketch decided, despite her exhaustion, to go there after work and check that Ashling and Sammy were okay.

The door to the staff room creaked open mid-afternoon and Jackie's head peered into the room.

"Hi. Begw said it was okay to come in."

"Hi. Of course. What are you doing here? Is everything okay?"

"Kind of. I need you to help me with something technical. Earlier I received an email from the inside of the computer. Can't tell you how relieved I am. They gave me this special account when I signed up and I'd forgotten all about it."

Sketch sat up, the pupils in her eyes expanding. "Is this about the device? Can they fix it?"

"They know something is wrong and are trying to fix it but they need to run some tests over the next few days. They want me to download some update for the computer and I've not a clue." Jackie handed Sketch a copy of the email. She read it letter by letter sensing a connection through the type to the world of her origin.

"Okay, the download can't be done on our computer. This is where the problem is. Can you do it at work?"

"'Fraid not. We're not allowed to download stuff, not since Rajid crashed the whole system with a rogue Trojan. Took days for them to get it operating again."

"Hmmm," said Sketch. She traced over the words with her fingers. "We could do it here. I've got the password."

"You won't get into any trouble?"

"I'm not supposed to use it for anything but library business but this is important, isn't it?"

"Yes," said Jackie. "We could ask one of my friends but I'd have to make up a story. Not like I can tell them the truth."

"The email says we need a USB stick. Have you got one?"

"Here," said Jackie holding up what looked like a Lego brick with a metal connector protruding out of the top.

The library was quiet and no one was booked. Together they booted up a PC and slid the brick into a USB slot. Sketch copied Jackie as she crossed her fingers.

The status monitor on the screen showed the download in progress.

"Thank goodness," said Jackie. "My next trick was to start praying, and I'm not sure it would make any difference given I don't believe in God."

Sketch glowed.

"Isn't it amazing how much fits into one of these tiny plastic things? When I started using a computer we had floppy disks to saving files on. They got corrupted for absolutely no reason."

A siren sounded on the streets outside the library. It registered with Sketch but the frequency of such alarms in London meant she thought little of it. A message appeared on the computer screen for Jackie. Both she and Sketch looked around to make sure no one could see what they were doing. The library was quiet, bar a huddle of people by the door. Whatever was happening, the timing of it was perfect.

They turned back to the computer, Sketch nervous to read it but keen for contact with the Core.

The download is complete. If you are seeing this the device should be working.

Jackie typed back quickly.

"How do you do it so fast?" Sketch asked her.

"Got a GCSE in typing. I'm a bit rusty. No one at work expects you to do anything quickly."

That's perfect thanks - such a relief. Sketch is doing well. She's a pleasure to be around.

Jackie smiled up at Sketch. She looked away blushing. Did Jackie really enjoy having her around?

Acceptable if surprising. We want to make sure the transformation will take place successfully should we choose to action it. To test this, you will send a small object to us. A pen or something similar.

Jackie rifled through her bag. "Can't find anything in this bag. Oh, how about this?" She pulled out an old, worn down lipstick. "I've been trying to get the remains out of it for weeks."

Place the item behind the tower and stand at least a metre away, like you did when we transformed Sketch.

Jackie and Sketch complied with the instructions.

Has it gone?

Sketch peered behind the computer and nodded to Jackie.

Yes, so where is the lipstick now?

The One replied a moment later.

We've transformed it into part of the browser. The bit used to make the colours. We thought it appropriate. Take the device out. Eject it from the screen. We will test again from your computer next week.

"You must be thrilled Sketch. I didn't want to say anything but I've been worried about what we'd do if it couldn't be fixed."

Sketch attempted a smile. "The One said, 'should we choose to action it.' It means they don't think I'm good enough to come back."

"You go on the way you have been and I don't doubt they'll take you back. I'll make sure of it," said Jackie winking.

Sketch hugged her, smelling the scent of warm human. It didn't matter what Jackie thought or said. In the end, it was up to her to prove she could do this. And it was down to the One to decide if she would be allowed to return to the Core.

Chapter 11

AFTER WORK, Sketch made her way to the estate where Ashling lived. She hadn't given any thought to what she would say when she arrived or what would happen if no one was in. It occurred to her she could call the police, but if no one answered how would she know if it was an emergency?

She reached Ashling's building and navigated her way to the correct intercom. The flat was on the second floor but she couldn't get through the front door unless someone buzzed her in. As she stood trying to raise the courage to press the button for Ashling's flat, someone breezed passed her, opening the door. She slid through the gap before it shut and made her way up the dark stairwell.

The door to the flat was identical to those on either side of it. Sketch took a deep breath, counted to three and knocked on the door. She pressed the doorbell, to be sure she would be heard, stood back and listened. A distant shuffling noise came from inside. It grew louder as a shadowy shape approached the door. As the door opened into the flat, light flooded in, revealing Ashling standing in the doorway.

"You're alive!" said Sketch. Ashling stared at her, a bewildered expression on her face.

"Yeh, always have been."

"I'm so pleased."

"Are you the girl from the library?"

"Yes, I knew you'd remember me. I've been so worried. I thought you were lying dead after choking on a chicken nugget," said Sketch who wanted to break into a dance. Ashling was alive!

"I'm a vegetarian." Ashling couldn't think of anything else to say. She began to edge the door closed but Sketch remained standing in front of her, grinning.

Ashling is alive kept running around her head on repeat.

"Why did you think I was dead?" asked Ashling.

"You didn't come to story time and you didn't add me as a friend on Facebook or Instagram. I sent you a message and you didn't reply, and I asked but no one has seen you for more than a week. I suppose I might have got a bit carried away."

"Sammy's had a cold and I'm skint, so we just stayed in," said Ashling. She shrugged. "It's how it is."

"I would have bought you a coffee at the library."

"That's kind but I hardly know you. I can't be taking things off you."

Sketch heard noises from down the corridor.

"Er, I've got to go and see to him. Do you want to come in?"

Sketch nodded. She was pleased to get out of the cold and happy Ashling wanted to talk more.

"You can wait in there," said Ashling pointing to a small room on the left. Sketch went into the living room. Her first impressions left her shocked at the stark contrast from the same room in Jackie's house. There was a ragged old sofa with a blanket thrown over it, a battered dining table and a couple of chairs. Opposite the sofa sat an old coffee table holding an old portable television set. The room was clean but lacked the extra touches to make it feel homely. The walls were littered with patches of peeling paint, and an area in the corner infected by damp contributed to the distinctive smell of mould. Sketch had never seen a home on the Internet or television that was as basic as this.

Through the thin walls, she made out the sounds of lots of

people speaking at once. They sounded aggressive and Sketch moved around the room at ill-ease in her new environment as she waited for Ashling to return.

"He's settled now. Can I get you a drink?"

"I'm alright," she said, conscious that Ashling was short of money.

"So, I'm still confused," the other woman said. "Why did you come round?"

Sketch shrugged. "Sounds silly now but I was worried about you. You vanished."

"Sometimes it's easier," said Ashling, folding up Sammy's clothes and putting them in a pile on the arm of the sofa.

"What do you mean?"

Ashling sat down and gestured to Sketch. She perched on the edge of a chair.

"At home, it's just me and Sammy. Outside, everyone seems all happy. Families out for the day, people in cafes drinking expensive drinks and eating food I could never afford on benefits. I end up feeling out of place, like I don't fit in anywhere anymore. I love Sammy but my life's changed since he arrived."

"He's a lovely boy." Sketch struggled for anything else to say, not used to awkward situations. The data downloaded to her comprised of factual information but she'd received no training in human emotions. Sadness and loneliness scared her, they might be infectious.

"Good news for libraries," she said, opting for happy news. Positive stories might make Ashling smile.

"A judge just ruled the closure of libraries in Gloucestershire and somewhere else is…" The details escaped her. "Well, they shouldn't close. Where would all the old people and poor people go? I read about it in the Independent newspaper." She saw Ashling suppress a smile.

My happy plan worked, she thought.

"Libraries are important but, to be honest, I'm more worried about cuts to benefits with the government and the economy being what it is. Babies are expensive. One day I'd like to go to college but right now the cost of childcare makes it impossible." Ashling picked at her fingers whilst Sketch searched in her head for another happy news story.

"So, how are you getting on at the library?" Ashling asked her.

"Oh, I love it–the people, the stories, the lives. I get sad at times, being away from home, but then I talk with the older people in my class and everyone at story time."

"I didn't realise you weren't from London."

"Really?"

"Totally – the way you speak is odd sometimes but no one sounds the same in a city this size."

Sketch felt a glow spread through her body, pleased to be accepted.

"You should get out a bit, spend time with people," said Sketch. "It will cheer you up. This girl, Rochelle, is throwing a party at her house on Saturday."

Ashling shook her head.

"I'm going with Matt. Dominic invited me and said I could bring some friends. Come with me."

"I can't Sketch," said Ashling.

"Go on. I could use the support. The thing is…I like Matt. I mean, I really like him but he likes Britney."

"I bet she doesn't like him," said Ashling snorting.

"Do you know Britney?" asked Sketch, edging her chair closer to the sofa.

"I know them all. They went to my school. Don't see them now."

"Oh," said Sketch. "Well, I've got a plan. When Britney rejects Matt at the party, I'll be there and he'll see me and realise I'm the one he really wants."

"Matt? You like Matt? Are you sure you've not been reading too many novels from the romance section?" said Ashling. Sketch played with the spikes in her hair.

"No, he's perfect for me. Please come."

"I can't even if I wanted to. I don't have anyone to take care of Sammy."

Life in your world

"Oh," said Sketch. The muscles in her face fell and then restored themselves. "What if I can find you a babysitter?"

"I don't know Sketch. I've never left him before, apart from a couple of hours during the day."

"What if I get you the most brilliant babysitter in London?" said Sketch.

Ashling bit her lip. "Maybe, but I could only go for a little while. No, it won't work."

"Why not?"

"It's going to sound stupid but I don't have any going-out clothes, nothing to wear."

No babysitter and lack of party clothes sounded like small hurdles to Sketch.

"Leave it to me," she said getting up from the chair. "Will you be here tomorrow afternoon?"

"Can't see where else I'd be."

"Okay, I'll come round at four and if I've not sorted out a babysitter you're happy with, but I will, I'll stay in with you and we can watch *The X Factor*," said Sketch.

"But…"

Sketch pretended to ignore Ashling as she left through the front door. "See you tomorrow Ashling. "Glad you are alive."

Chapter 12

SKETCH NOW FACED the difficult task of coming up with a babysitter as she didn't intend to miss Rochelle's party. She'd spent a long time planning what she would say to Matt after Britney broke his heart, and she was also looking forward to meeting Dominic. An online friendship had developed between them. The process of their communications reminded her of the way energies meet with ease. Dominic was funny; he knew what words to use to make her laugh, how to cheer her up and messaging him made her feel good about herself.

Operation Ashling hinged on two things, the most important being the need to find someone willing to sit in her house and make sure nothing bad happened to Sammy.

This was a perfect opportunity to match up Maud, her family being far away, and Ashling, who appeared to have no family or friends at all, she thought.

Next only to the scheme to get Matt to fall for her, this was the most brilliant thing she'd ever thought of.

She knew where Maud lived without having to break the confidentiality of her placement at the library. The old lady had written down her address for Sketch, telling her to pop round anytime she wanted too. Sketch had assured her she would come to visit for a cuppa soon. She loved Maud's company, with her wisdom, kindness and ready smile. Her new computer bought by her son in Australia would be arriving in the next few days and Sketch offered to come round and ensure it was properly installed. Maud was so excited at the prospect of showing off her IT skills to her antipodean family and how wonderful it would be to see their faces when she used Skype to call them.

Early Saturday morning, eager to ask Maud for her help, Sketch wolfed down her breakfast.

"Don't get there before nine," said Jackie. "I know old people don't sleep as much but she might still be in her bed."

She held on until nine thirty before she found herself knocking on Maud's door. Sketch admired the way Maud maintained the paint working. She knew the older lady had lived in the house for years and, although the council owned it, she viewed it as her own.

There was no reply and not a sound from inside the house. She knocked again thinking perhaps Maud had problems hearing things. She'd heard this was common in older people as their ears deteriorated with age. Still no response came from Maud, so Sketch bent down to the letterbox.

"Maud, it's me Sketch. Are you in?"

Getting no response, Sketch concluded Maud was shopping or to visiting one of the other people in the Silver Surfers group. For a moment Sketch imagined Maud collapsed and inside needing to be rescued. Then she remembered how worried she'd been about Ashling and how she had turned out to be okay. Aware she should keep her vivid imagination in check, Sketch rationalised there would be a normal, sensible explanation for Maud's failure to answer the door.

She decided to go off and find something for Ashling to wear to the party. She'd raked through her own wardrobe but nothing would fit her new friend. Ashling was a little rounder than Sketch and also shorter at five feet. Sketch's other problem was a lack of money. What Jackie had given her wouldn't go far, even in the cheapest clothes shops. There was Primarni, a massive, bargain basement shop selling on-trend clothing designed only to be worn two or three times. The nearest store was on Oxford Street meaning a journey on the tube, changing trains as she went. But Begw had told her to avoid the place at all costs on as it was a Mecca for tourists, ranking high on the tourist attractions alongside Buckingham Palace, The Tower of London and the London Eye.

The alternative to getting Ashling's outfit together was to scour the numerous charity shops in the area. Some of them would sometimes be hiding a real bargain, designer clothing, homemade gems or stunning accessories at affordable prices. They would be the place to locate the perfect getup for Ashling. After rummaging through a couple of different charity shops, she found some denim shorts and a sparkling black and gold top she could match with a pair of black tights.

Party clothes ticked off the list, Sketch returned to Maud's front door but found she was still not in. Running out of time and holding the bag of party clothes she couldn't return was going to be pretty useless if she didn't have a babysitter for Sammy. She dashed back to her house and explained everything to Jackie.

"Pleeeeeeeasee, pleeeeease, pleeeeease, Jackie. She's not been out for two years. Two *whole* years. Can you imagine that?"

"I'm not so old I can't remember having a small child, even if the details are fuzzy."

"So will you do it? Will you come and Sammy sit?"

"As long as he's going to be in bed when I get there. I guess it'll be no different to staying in and watching TV. I want you all back by one in the morning."

Sketch yelped, hugged Jackie and dashed off towards the front door. "Thank you, thank you, thank you. I'm going to go and tell Ashling now."

Ashling remained apprehensive, both at the thought of leaving Sammy and a night out.

"But you said you've met Jackie at a parents' evening at school."

"When I was in year eight. I said 'hello' and gave her Matt's report. I'm still not sure. Sammy doesn't know her. What if he wakes up and gets upset?"

"Ashling, you said you would go if I got you something to wear and a babysitter, and I've got you both. Plus, Jackie is a whiz with kids," said Sketch hoping this was true.

"Maybe."

"I'll have my phone with me and you can use it to phone Jackie whenever you like."

Ashling laughed. "I don't suppose you are going to let me stay in, are you?"

Sketch shook her head vigorously.

"I'd best get my hair washed and do something with my face, then."

"Brilliant," said Sketch unable to stop her smile from spreading across the full extent of her face. "We'll be round at eight."

Chapter 13

"WOW," said Jackie taking in Sketch's party get up. Her short off-the-shoulder gold shimmery dress and the pair of heels she wore made her appear taller than the avatar she'd transformed into.

"Do I look okay?" she asked.

"You look much more than okay. You're gorgeous. Go and stand with Matt so I can get a photo of you both," said Jackie.

The two sidled up next to each other, Sketch tottering in her high heels and Matt in his best jeans and t-shirt.

"Matt, put your arm round Sketch then," said Jackie.

Matt looked at Sketch and raised his eyebrow but did as instructed reminding Sketch of the time they hugged.

With photos taken, they gathered their belongings ready to go and Matt carried with him a fabric charity bag containing the bottles of wine Jackie had given them to take to the party on the understanding they would just drink these or beer and not any hard spirits.

"Ignore me at your peril," she said.

Ashling opened the door to the trio and smiled. "Hello. Come in. Please, excuse the mess."

"Hi, Ashling. I'm Jackie." Ashling took the hand held out to her and shook it.

"It's lovely to meet you. Now I don't want you to worry at all. Go out and have a good time," said Jackie.

Ashling attempted a smile.

"Honestly, hon. Little Sammy will be fine. Show me his room, where everything is and I promise I'll text you on the hour so you know we're both okay," said Jackie.

"Do you like the clothes?" asked Sketch. "You are stunning in those shorts, isn't she, Matt?"

Matt grunted a sort of nondescript answer indicating neither a yes nor a no. Sketch noticed Ashling's face turn a little red at the compliment and presumed she wasn't used to people saying nice things about her, making a mental note to be extra kind to her new friend.

After a list of instructions about sleeping, favourite stories, nappies, drinks and how to work the TV, Jackie shooed them all out of the flat with renewed promises to text on an hourly basis, sneaking in another photo before they left, this time of the three of them together.

The party was at a house in Kentish Town about twenty minutes walk away from Ashling's home. The conversation between them was stilted. Sketch did her best to think of things to talk about they all had in common.

"I loved that Hawkeye comic you left in the living room."

"S'all right," said Matt. "Can lend you some more if you are interested?"

Sketch noticed a blank look on Ashling's face.

"Do you like our outfits?"

Changing the subject had no effect. The aim of the night was to show Matt how witty, interesting, and attractive she was. Instead, he replied in grunts.

"That must be Rochelle's house," said Sketch. Even before they reached it, loud music with a strong pulsating bass could be heard as they walked down the road. Matt puffed up like a peacock as they approached. Sketch took Ashling's arm, smiling at her. She was more excited than the other two could possibly imagine as they were unaware she'd never been to a party before. She'd seen the pictures and everything looked so sparkly and fun on Facebook. Lots of smiling people, likes and comments. Aside from a few drunken people, parties were brilliant, according to the Internet.

A small group of teenagers huddled, smoking outside. The group looked them up and down as they passed by before going back to their conversation. No one seemed bothered as they walked into the house. All their efforts to secure an invitation seemed to have been superfluous. They could have turned up without anyone challenging them.

"I'm off to find Britney," said Matt dashing off with a bottle of wine.

Sketch and Ashling pushed their way through the throngs of people chatting, dancing and snogging. In the corner, illegal drugs were being consumed. Sketch knew it was against the law and she'd get into trouble if she got caught taking them, but the fact they made people happy, alert and could be hallucinogenic intrigued her. Music pounded in their ears, making hearing difficult unless they shouted to each other.

"Let's find Dominic," mouthed Sketch.

Ashling couldn't make out what she said but nodded and followed her through the throngs of inebriated teenagers. Accompanying the loud sounds of music and shouting were intense smells, perfumes, alcohol, sweat, and pheromones. The lingering smell of smoke swirled around the room, mingling with words and adding to the party's atmosphere. Sketch stored them in her memory.

It took ten minutes to find Dominic, during which time Sketch tried to make herself seen by as many people as possible whilst Ashling did her best attempt at invisibility. A number of old classmates recognised Ashling but turned away when she tried to speak to them.

"I shouldn't have come," she muttered.

"What?" said Sketch.

"Nothing."

Sketch was oblivious to her friend's discomfort. She continued to shoot around the house, introducing herself and asking where Dominic was. After a couple of failed attempts to locate him, involving a trip to the kitchen and a journey to the cupboard under the stairs, they found Dominic in his bedroom, glued to an Xbox, intent on shooting the hell out of some faceless baddy.

"Hi," shouted Sketch. Dominic didn't move apart from the rapid movement of his fingers on a games controller.

"Dominic."

"He's got earphones in," said Ashling pointing at the sides of her head. "He can't hear you."

Sketch strode over had removed an earpiece from the hole in his head.

"Hi, Dominic. It's me."

"Sketch?" said Dominic, looking around in alarm. "Ashling?"

"Yes. Correct. Well done. Why are you hiding up here in your room when we should be downstairs partying?" asked Sketch. "It's your party after all."

"Not really, it's my sister's. I promised to keep out of the way."

"Yeh, but we're all dressed up for a party and I want to talk to you. Your room doesn't smell so great," said Sketch pinching her nostrils.

Ashling poked her in the side.

"No offence. I mean you must be used to it but my nose isn't, so can we go and get a drink?"

"I'm not sure," said Dominic still holding on to the games controller. "This is the first time I've gotten to this level."

Ashling and Sketch exchanged looks.

"Wrong answer," said Sketch, taking the plastic controller from him and ending the game.

"What've you done?"

"You've got to join us now."

"I really don't think this is a good idea," he said.

Ashling laughed.

"What's the joke?"

"That's what I said to Sketch and here I am standing in your bedroom. You've no hope when you live in the house where the party is happening."

Sketch nodded. "You're coming with us if we have to drag you away from your smelly room. Fancy not wanting to spend time with us. Look how gorgeous we are." She twirled around reminding herself of life in the Core.

He sighed. "Alright then, you've wrecked this game so I might as well duck out."

Sketch was surprised. Dominic seemed different in real life from his online persona. In his house, amidst the party, he seemed smaller and a little dull. It wasn't even as if he appeared to be shy, just that he was missing the spark he had when they chatted online. She tried making a joke about comics but he looked at her as if she was some strange being.

"Beer!" said Sketch. She'd recovered enough from her first scrape with teenage alcohol poisoning to have another go at drinking. She still couldn't even sniff cider without the memory of her head down the loo and a churning stomach, but beer sounded doable. She grabbed three cans, handed two to her friends, opened the remaining one and sipped.

"Umm, much better than cider, this."

Dominic and Ashling smiled at each other seeing Sketch's quirky enthusiasm.

"Oh look, there they are." As she saw Matt and Britney across the room, she stopped unable to move or talk.

In a movie, the crowds in the room would have parted leaving no one in the line of sight between her, Matt and Britney. In reality, all kinds of people stood in the way; tall, welding large haircuts, or bouncing up and down in the appearance of some kind of dance. She could see bits of Matt's head and sections of Britney's. In particular, the proximity of their mouths and noses. Far from having rejected Matt, Britney was engaged in a full on snog, with tongues and a little groping of bumpier body parts.

"Sketch," said Ashling seeing her friend drop her can of beer and run off towards the garden. She chased after the tall, skinny blond girl as she disappeared behind a door.

"Sketch, stop. Matt's an idiot. He really is."

She stopped waiting for a response and then Ashling heard movement from behind the door. A latch lifted up and from out of the darkness came the outline of Sketch's head.

"Quick, get in," she said, pulling Ashling into the black interior of the abandoned outdoor toilet.

"Shall I get my phone out? It's got a torch app."

"No," said Sketch. "I like it like this. I don't want to see anything. I want to go blind rather than see them two…" She paused. "Kissing." She choked as she spoke and started to cry.

Ashling pulled a hankie from her bag.

"Here, blow your nose and have some beer. They aren't worth crying about. Britney's a nasty piece of work and Matt, well Matt has never been able to see what was right in front of his face."

Sketch blew hard into the tissue; amazed she had yet again produced so much liquid from inside her head. Why wasn't it all used up after last Sunday's session of hysteria? That had been about Matt, too. Matt was supposed to make her happy.

"Right now he's just making you bloody miserable," said Ashling as Sketch told her what she was thinking.

The two sat and sipped on the shared can of beer.

"Are you going to let Matt spoil my only night out in—"

"Two years," said Sketch.

The two laughed.

"No one's finished my sentence in years," Ashling told her.

"No, I guess not," said Sketch. "But won't everyone laugh at me if we go back in?"

"They won't care. Most of them won't even speak to me 'cause of Sammy. I think they think having a baby is contagious."

Ashling dug into her bag and retrieved her phone. She checked for her text from Jackie. After sending a reply, she turned on the phone's torch app and pointed the light towards Sketch's face. It wasn't too blotchy but some emergency repairs could be done to her eye makeup as the mascara had been swept down her face by the earlier torrent of tears.

With eyes fixed, they went in search of another beer and found Dominic waiting for them by the kitchen door.

"You alright?" he asked.

"Yup, but I've lost my beer," said Sketch managing to smile a little. "What's a party without beer?"

Dominic popped into the kitchen and took a bottle from the puddle of water that had once been a pile of ice in the sink.

"Thanks Dominic."

The effort of talking lessened after a drink, their inhibitions fading. They sat on the front doorstep watching local people pass by, and counting how many cigarettes the hardened smokers could burn away in an hour.

"So, your baby is named Sammy?" asked Dominic.

"Not so much of a baby now. He's almost two, and he'll be able to go to nursery soon," said Ashling.

"I can't imagine being with a baby all the time. Doesn't it drive you mental?"

"Yes, sometimes. But you know, I love him in a way I could never have imagined before I got pregnant. Everyone says that but it's true."

"Do they?" asked Dominic. "You're the first person I know that's had a baby."

Sketch laughed. "Me too."

"What you laughing about?" asked Ashling.

"It's just funny," she said.

"Sketch?" said Dominic.

"Yeh?"

"Where did you live before? I mean, you just sort of arrived from nowhere. Where is home?"

Ashling and Dominic turned to face Sketch.

Not knowing what to say so kept as close to the truth as she could.

"Home is far away. Things had been difficult and I didn't have a job so they thought I would benefit from some time away somewhere different," she said.

"So you're from the country?" asked Ashling.

"Well, it's very different, where I come from. I love Tufnell Park, though, and want to see more London whilst I'm here."

"Sketch, you are going to think I've gone totally mad but this geezer Harry or summit, on Facebook, said you'd been in prison."

Sketch spluttered out her mouthful of beer.

"What?"

"Sorry, I shouldn't have said anything but I'm a bit drunk and I just wanted to make sure, I can't imagine you being locked up," said Dominic.

Both Ashling and Dominic stared at Sketch.

"No, I've never been in prison. Fancy someone saying that," she began to giggle. "It's like saying I've come from inside your computer."

"Yeh, completely nuts, eh?" said Dominic. "Sorry, it was a stupid thing to say."

"What's strange is that someone would say it to you Dominic," said Ashling.

Dominic insisted on walking them back to the flat after checking first that Matt didn't want to go with them. Sketch was glad he wasn't coming back yet as her housemate was the last person she wanted to see. She guessed Matt was still entwined with Britney when Dominic returned without him.

Chapter 14

MATT DIDN'T arrive home until the early hours of the morning and then headed straight for his room via the kitchen. Sketch heard him going through the cupboards and suspected he'd loaded up with snacks and fizzy drinks. He didn't appear the next morning for breakfast.

"I'm not happy with him, Sketch," said Jackie. "He promised to come home with you girls, and now I find out he's lied to his dad. He's said he can't go over today because of an assignment."

"Maybe he does have an essay to write," said Sketch.

"You do like to see the good in people, don't you?"

"Yeh. Is that bad?"

"No, it's one of the many things about you that I love. I spoke to the One this morning. I've told it…is it male or female?" asked Jackie stirring a pan of porridge.

"Neither," said Sketch. "It doesn't work the same in the Core. The One doesn't have a gender. Operational energies are assigned genders so as to experience human diversity."

"Oh, how refreshing. Anyway, we communicated and I've told it how you've progressed since you've been with us."

"Really?" Sketch's face showed signs of genuine surprise.

"Yes, really. You've learnt a lot about being human."

"But I've so much left to discover and it's nearly time to go home," said Sketch.

"You've got ages left to go. It's amazing what can happen in a short time."

"I thont lik thad Bridnee," she said through a mouthful of toast.

Jackie laughed. "Try again when you've chewed Sketch. I didn't hear a word."

Sketch ground down on the contents of her mouth and swallowed. "I don't like that Britney, you know, Matt's new girlfriend."

"Boys of Matt's age, well they like a different girl every week. Having said that, do you really want to get involved with him and then have to go back in a couple of weeks?"

Sketch hadn't thought about it like that before. She'd been so busy trying to make him fall in love with her that she'd not seen beyond the first kiss. Well maybe a little further, but certainly not past the first night.

"I suppose not," she said. "But I still don't like her. She says things like 'do one' and then doesn't explain to do one what."

"Another one of those expressions we use that make no sense," said Jackie.

"Jackie, how did you know I liked Matt?" asked Sketch.

"When you get to be my age, you just know some things."

"Do you think he knows?"

"I shouldn't think so. Another thing about teenage boys is if you don't tell them something straight to their face, then they'll be oblivious. So what have you got planned for next week?"

"Just the library, and I want to go and see Maud. I left her a note yesterday cause she was out," said Sketch.

"Good idea," said Jackie finishing up her tea. "Invite her round for dinner next Sunday. Matt will be out so it will be just you, me and Maud."

The thought of Maud's face when she invited her round for Sunday lunch cheered Sketch. "Brilliant. Can I invite Ashling and Sammy too?"

"Why not? The more the merrier," Jackie replied.

Life in your world

By Monday morning Sketch had regained some of her sparkle. She resolved to forget about Matt and her misjudged feelings for him, but it was impossible to switch off her feelings overnight. Knowing he was in the kitchen brewing up some tea she made sure her make-up was on and her face displayed a smile before making her way downstairs.

"Hi, Matt," she said squeezing past him trying to avoid their bodies colliding with each other.

"Thanks for getting me invited to the party. I'm well in with Britney now," said Matt ruffling her hair and finding spiky gel points meet his fingers instead of the fluffy white hair he was expecting.

"You're welcome," she said grabbing a cereal bar from the cupboard on her way through to the dining area. She wanted to check online before heading off to work having discovered her phone was out of battery.

She'd not spoken to Dominic since the party but they had exchanged messages on Sunday. He had been round to see Ashling and the two of them had taken Sammy out for a trip to Hampstead Heath. He seemed happy but much less keen to chat than before.

Dominic's message said he'd posted the photos from the party so they could all see them. Logging on, Sketch saw herself, captured in digital form. She was tagged, her face on all the pictures. She looked stunning, even after the crying incident. A couple of images made her wince but all-in-all she was pleased with Dominic's album. In addition to the photos, she had five new friend requests, all from people she'd met at the weekend, except one. It was from a strange young man named Harry.

His name sounds familiar, she thought, but she hadn't seen him at the party.

Still, many of the teenagers looked the same to her – he must be one of them. With little time before she had to leave for work, Sketch clicked accept to all of her requests and shutdown the computer.

"Oi, Sketch, I was going to use that," said Matt. Sketch shrugged her shoulders and headed off to the library with a smirk on her face.

Chapter 15

THE MORNING WAS FOGGY, which made it difficult to see far ahead when walking down the road. Sketch's local knowledge had grown. She smiled at familiar faces at bus stops, bought a coffee at Bean Around Town, and popped into Greggs. Sketch arrived at work, sausage sarnie in hand, looking forward to an easy day of shelving and chatting away to the library regulars who came to the building seeking refuge from the boredom of unemployment, retirement and the rising costs of staying warm in your own home. Begw was opening up as she arrived.

"Hi, Sketch. How was your weekend?" she asked pulling up the metal shutters.

"Good thanks. I've given up boys. They're just trouble."

"So it's girls for you, now, is it?" said Begw. Sketch thought she saw her boss wink but couldn't be sure it wasn't a twitch.

"No, that's not what I meant. I like girls but not like that," said Sketch.

"Hiya, Sketch. How was the party? Did you get to snog the marvellous Matt?" Trevor breezed in through the door behind them.

"Sketch has decided to join my side," said Begw sticking her tongue out at Trevor.

"No, I haven't," said Sketch. "I'm just mad at Matt cos he went off with Britney."

"Oh my days," said Trevor. "Sounds like quite a weekend."

"*Panad?*" asked Sketch, trying to change the subject.

"No time for that young'un. We've got a war to wage and we're having a meeting before we let anyone in this morning," said Begw. Trevor and Sketch exchanged curious glances.

Images of guns, bombs, and rationing ran through Sketch's mind. She'd watched the news last night and there'd been little sign of conflict and nothing big enough to spin the country into warfare overnight.

"They think they can close us down. They're wrong. They've chosen the wrong Welsh librarian to do battle with."

"Err...*who* wants to close us down?" asked Trevor getting his question in before Sketch could ask hers.

Begw stared at them both as if they were stupid.

"Did you not get my memo?" Her voice took on a lilting Welsh aspect, her eyes narrowed. Sketch resisted an urge to hide behind Trevor.

"No, I..."

"The council. The council wants to shut down the library."

"Have you thought about sending them a harsh letter of complaint? That often does the trick. Got me a free vacuum cleaner last year," said Trevor.

"I suspect this time we need more than a letter," said Begw. "So I sent a memo. To you both."

Sketch had heard of memos. They were notes circulated to members of staff in offices usually by bosses and often bearing ill tidings. They'd become redundant with the spread of the Internet and email.

"A memo? I didn't get a memo," said Sketch, feeling somewhat left out.

"It wasn't an actual memo. What do you think this is? 1986?" said Begw. "I emailed everyone.

"What I'm about to tell you, you can't tell anyone else," she continued. "Or I'll lose my job."

"Sounds like you're going to lose it anyway, darling," said Trevor.

Begw glared at him. "Get the kettle on now. We need to decide what to do to put a stop to this."

During the day, the time thief crept in and stole hours from the clock. Ashling and Sammy joined them for the story time session. Sketch saw a change in Ashling who, though still reserved, was interacting more with the other parents. More mums and tots turned up this week. Whilst this made no difference financially to the library, larger user numbers gave them more ammunition in the battle against closure.

Chapter 16

SKETCH PLANNED to go around to Maud's at the end of the day to invite her for Sunday lunch. After story time, she took her break in the small staff room and continued reading a Young Adult novel about vampires she'd started the previous week. The story was simple but compelling. Against all odds, it made the blood-sucking creatures of the night sound attractive. Her mind was in the world of the story so she failed to notice Begw enter the room.

"Sketch," she said.

"Am I late back from my break?" asked Sketch, putting down the book without saving her page.

"No. Sketch, I think you should sit down."

Sketch gave her boss a quizzical look and then stared at the chair. Was she missing something? Why was Begw sounding so odd?

"Oh, you are sitting down. Well then maybe I should sit down, then," said Begw moving down onto the cushioned chair. The pair looked at each other. Sketch wasn't sure if she was supposed to say anything.

"Is this about the closure? I'm sure we can fight it," Sketch told Begw.

"Sketch, do you remember last week when you were on the computer with Jackie?"

Sketch nodded. "I'm sorry, I know it was jittery but it was important and no one needed me."

"It's not that," Begw stopped and lowered her head. "There was an accident outside with sirens, an ambulance and all that. I didn't know who it was."

"What? Who was it?" asked Sketch.

"Oh Sketch. It was…it was Maud."

"Maud? Is she okay?" said Sketch concerned and frightened for the old lady.

"No Sketch, she's not okay. She was hit by a car head on. There was nothing anyone could do to help her." Begw reached over to take her hand but Sketch pulled it away.

"Where is she? What hospital is she in? I'm going to go and see her now." Sketch refusing to listen to what Begw was telling her.

"Sketch, no. You can't go and see her. Maud is dead."

Sketch grabbed her coat from the row of pegs and ran out. For the second time in two days something had upset her enough to run off, but this time it was different, it was serious, not just about some stupid boy. This time her friend was dead.

I know all about death, she thought. *I've read about it, the human ending. When your current form wore itself out, you transformed into a newer energy force or being.*

It was the cycle of life, never stopping because of sadness and grief. Death was a natural, beautiful phenomenon. In the Core they believed it to be so. There was light in change. Now everything she'd learnt and believed in was revealed to be a lie. If it had been true, why was she gripped with an all-encompassing pain? Powerful emotions and physical sensations overwhelmed her.

The truth was the world was cruel and ugly.

The sun had burnt off the gloom of the winter fog but Sketch failed to register the weather. The day remained dark as she journeyed, as if her eyes were shut, through the streets of North London, not seeing the flowers left on the roadside by the library in memory of her fallen friend. Silent tears rolling from her eyes without the strength of weeping to force them downwards, but still they fell.

She walked on autopilot, finding herself outside the Kentish Town tube station. Not wanting to go home or back to the library, she took the escalator down into the sculptured earth and jumped on the first Northern line train stopping at the southbound platform.

A list of things she'd planned to do with Maud before returning to the Core popped up and faded, like space dust in her head - drinking coffee, dinner Jackie, Ashling and Sammy, teaching her to Skype so she could speak to her family in Australia. They would never see her again. Never hear her voice.

The train navigated the southward route under the Thames. Sketch gave no thought to where she might be going. The destination was unimportant. What mattered was that she was moving, and moving meant doing something. Standing still made things go awry, but if she kept moving everything would be okay.

Except, she thought, *it wouldn't be.*

The tube terminated at Kennington, forcing Sketch to make a decision. She could stay on the underground and return to Tufnell Park or get off in the south and wander the streets. An urge was building in her to hit someone and, not used to such strong, violent emotions, she left the train. She would find somewhere quiet to be, move around, and process.

Rain plummeted down from a grey winter sky as she left the station, making it impossible for Sketch to distinguish between the tears rolling down her face and the drops of water pouring from the dark clouds above. The exterior of the station provided nowhere to sit so she began to walk, paying no attention to her route or the passing landmarks. Thirty minutes later, finding herself soaked to the skin and without a clue to where she was, she stopped. A spiral of questions poked their way into her mind and refused to leave. Had someone held Maud's hand as she died? Had the police arrested the person who knocked her to her death? Were her family coming? Sketch needed to talk to her family, to tell them how much Maud wanted to

Skype with them. Maud would want them to know. She must tell them.

Clothes and hair soaked, cold and unsure of her location, Sketch headed for the nearest bus stop. She tried to work out how to get back to the tube but the station wasn't showing on the map at the bus stop. A bus she thought was going in the right direction drew up. It was dry, unlike the street where the rain was unrelenting and would bring some relief from the weather. She put her hand in her pocket. Empty space filled the place where her oyster card should have been. She scrambled around in her bag. It had to be there. Everyone on the bus was staring at her, she was sure, all the passengers frustrated they couldn't move on because a bedraggled rag doll of a girl had lost her means of payment. She wanted to shout at them, "Maud is dead! Do you not care?"

She stepped off onto the pavement and into a puddle, its contents seeping into her shoes. She couldn't find her oyster card and already knew she'd spent all her money that morning. She stood in the rain crying, engulfed by a loneliness she'd never experience in either the human world or in the inside of the computer.

"Are you alright, love?" asked a short, balding man.

"No," sniffed Sketch. "I'm lost and my oyster has gone and Maud is dead."

"Where you going?"

"Tufnell Park, I've got no money," she said between sobs, embarrassed to admit this, and worried she sounded like a beggar.

"You got a mobile? Can you call someone?"

Sketch nodded and looked for her phone finding it in the mysterious black hole of the large bag. She'd turned it off when she exited the tube ignoring a number of missed calls from Begw, Trevor, Jackie and Ashling.

The phone sprung to life again as she switched it on, with a flurry of messages alerting her to voicemails. She didn't have much credit or the inclination to listen to them all so she just selected Jackie's number and let the phone dial her guardian.

"Jackie, it's me. I'm lost in south London and my oyster has gone and…" Sketch began to cry again.

"It's alright. We'll get you home," said Jackie.

The man at the bus stop waved a fiver in her face.

"I'll show you how to get to the northern line. This will get you back."

"Thank you," said Sketch managing a small smile, grateful for his help but not happy at all.

"Sketch?" said Jackie.

"S'ok, I'm here. A nice man is going to help me. He's given me some money."

"Ok, well get his address and I'll make sure he gets it back. You okay to get on the tube? I'll meet you at the other end," said Jackie.

"Yeh, I'll be alright."

"Sure? I can come down there but it will take a little while," said Jackie.

"I'm sure. I just want to come home now. I'm so sad," said Sketch sniffing the runny liquids intent on escaping from her nose.

"I know, hon, I know. You'll be back here in no time."

The journey back appeared longer than the trip south to Kennington. Sketch focused on adverts and poems on the walls of the tube carriage. She read each word slowly, squinting to see the small print, normally never read by the average passenger. She ran out of words and wished she had a book to lose herself in. She loved that about books, the way you could be so engrossed in the story that you were temporarily transported to a different world where fictional people were real and you were an onlooker to their life. She needed that right now, to blank out the persistent and painful thoughts of Maud and the fact she was no longer alive.

After forty minutes and two delays to regulate the service, Sketch emerged from the station into the darkening skies of Tufnell Park. She ran to Jackie, allowing herself to be folded into the safety of her arms, surrendering responsibility for herself to the older woman.

"She's...Maud, she's..." Sketch tried to speak.

"Shhh, now. I know, I know. Let's get you back to the house," said Jackie.

Chapter 17

SKETCH FLOATED through the next day, fractured and disconnected from the human world around her. She spent most of it in her pyjamas, unshowered, watching programmes on daytime television that didn't register with her. Internally, she attempted to process her feelings, to understand what humans called grief – the loss of those close or important to you. Her happy memories of Maud were tainted by her death as if someone had dragged a muddy rag across a priceless piece of art.

Thinking of the woman triggered sadness, a physical hollowness that made eating impossible, and surging, hot anger seemed to explode from nowhere. She curled up under a blanket, arms crossed over her chest holding it in. Jackie tried to reassure her but the words skimmed across her mind, not settling or sinking deep enough to give any real comfort. At the same time Sketch wouldn't let Jackie leave the house, finding her presence comforting.

The second morning after finding out about Maud's death Sketch came down to the kitchen, showered and dressed. She sat facing Jackie across the table.

"Maud really wanted to see her family. They should know that," she said. Her words were mumbled. "I want to meet them, but they're in Australia."

Jackie looked at the sad young woman sitting in her kitchen.

"I suspect they'll be coming over for the funeral. It's a long way but for things like this, people normally fly back as soon as they can," said Jackie. "I'll see what I can find out."

Despite Maud having lived in the area for years, it proved difficult to find out anything about her family. Jackie visited her neighbours in the evening but most of them had moved to the area in recent months and didn't know Maud. She contacted the council who were also trying to trace her family because they needed to clear her belongings from the house. Sketch's energy levels dipped after each time Jackie's attempts to find Maud's family failed. She dragged herself around the house wondering if the life of a stone energy was without pain or emotion.

Jackie returned home on Wednesday evening to find Sketch staring out the window.

"Good news," she said.

Sketch doubted that. Maud was still gone. Everyone she knew would die, they would all leave grieving friends and family.

"I popped into the surgery on my way home. Turns out they've got contacts for Maud's family."

"Really?" asked Sketch turning away from her view of the garden.

"Yes, the nurse promised to pass on my details to them. She said they are flying out to make the arrangements."

"Can I meet them?"

"That depends on them," said Jackie. "I'm sure they'll want you to come to the funeral and pay your respects."

Sketch returned to work at the library on Thursday morning, to enormous hugs from Trevor. Begw, not being a very huggy person made up for it with cups of tea and a welcome back sausage.

"I told the other oldies, the Silver Surfers group, about Maud," said Begw.

"Were they upset?"

"Sad, I'd say, but by the time you get to their age, they've lost a few people."

"Does that make it easier?" asked Sketch.

"Think it still hurts, but not like the first time," said Begw shrugging her shoulders. "Bought them all teas instead of doing computer stuff, so they could talk about it together."

During the day some members of the Silver Surfers group popped into see Sketch. They booked time on the computers, asking her questions.

"Best to stay busy," said Mrs Edgar-Harrington after making Sketch send replies to four emails.

At lunchtime, Sketch found Begw in the staffroom.

"There's something I want to do next week. It's really important. I think Maud wants me to do it," said Sketch. She was going to do it anyway but she would at least go through the motions of asking her boss.

"Go on Sketch, tell me more."

Sketch shared her idea, explaining why it was important.

Begw nodded. "Great idea. I really like it. I think we can combine your plans with the campaign to stop the closure of the library." The librarian outlined the scheme she had been plotting with Trevor in Sketch's absence.

"Can I leave it to you then?" asked Begw.

"Yes," said Sketch. "I'll sort it."

She spent the rest of the day focused on work tasks, remembering Maud telling her to just take one thing at a time if she was having a bad day. At the time they'd had the conversation, Sketch couldn't have comprehended having a truly bad day, but now her worldview had shifted, tilting on its axis. As she reflected on Maud's advice, she sensed an enduring link to the woman and the words she'd left behind to guide her.

Chapter 18

THE HOUSE WAS empty when Sketch returned from work. She found a scribbled note left by Jackie on the kitchen table, explaining she would be back at six thirty and asking Sketch not to go out.

Fine, thought Sketch who had no plans to go anywhere.

She logged onto the Internet hoping either Dominic or Harry was online for her to chat to. Harry, it turned out lived in another area of the country. She'd not met him at Rochelle's party. He said he'd seen her photos from the party and thought she looked cute. As she was only in the outer world for a few more weeks she couldn't see any harm in chatting online to him. She was not going to physically meet him so there was no chance he would end up being a completely different person – his existence for her would be limited to the Internet.

Her online friends were a good distraction from what was going on in real life. She put on a mask to communicate with them, a smiling plastic mask covering her sadness about Maud, and when she'd had enough for the day she could take it off and disappear.

Harry showed as online.

Hi Sketch. You surviving in that London?

Hey Harry. It's brilliant, the whole world in one city.

They rude in London. That's what I heard. Not as friendly as where I am.
You're only saying that cos you've never been here.
True, but you've not been there long yourself.

Sketch didn't remember telling Harry about her temporary living arrangement but once you were on the Internet everyone could find out everything about you, from what you had for dinner the night before to what you scored in primary school tests.

Everyone I've met has been lovely. This week I got lost in the middle of south London and this complete stranger helped me out. He made sure I got home.

LOL, he was probs a Northerner.

Like you? Are you a Northerner then Harry?

Depends on where you're standing.

She continued to argue her point with Harry but he refused to back down or concede that people could be connected to one another in a large city like London. The door open and closed, and Sketch heard the sound of footsteps belonging to various owners travelling along the landing above. Down the stairs came four sets of legs. Jackie's jeans arrived first, followed closely by the legs of a man and woman, and a teenager about the same age as Matt.

"Hi," said Sketch getting up from the computer.

"Sketch, this is John, Sarah and Martin. They're Maud's family. They flew in today," explained Jackie.

"Oh," said Sketch. This must be what Sammy feels like when he's put in a room full of adults he's never seen before. "Hi." She held her hand out towards him, remembering the conventions of humans.

"Hello, Sketch, I hope you don't mind us descending on you like this," said John.

She shook her head.

"Jackie said it would be okay. She told us how very kind you've been…were to mum. Mum talked nonstop about you on the phone. We spoke to her…" John stopped. Sketch noticed Sarah squeeze his arm.

"We rang Maud a couple of days before she passed," said his wife. "You did amazing things for her."

"I was just her teacher," said Sketch mumbling. She couldn't say thank you and was unsure how to deal with the praise given to her.

"You were much more than that," said John. "You brought a spark of something into her life. She'd perked up to no end. Everyone could see it."

"We can't thank you enough for being her friend. I've been so guilty about how lonely she was. I even offered to fly her out to live with us but she wouldn't have it, so to know she had someone looking out for her before she died means so much to us."

"Australia's so far away," said Sarah.

"I know what you mean. She wanted to be able to talk to you more. You know she was learning it all so she could Skype you?" said Sketch.

"We do," said Martin, speaking for the first time. "She sent me an email. Did she tell you?"

Sketch shook her head.

"She must have sent it from the library because she never got the computer we ordered for her."

"We just wanted you to know how proud she was so proud of it. She said she couldn't have done it without you," said John with a sad smile.

Sketch wanted to hug him. It probably wasn't the right thing to do but she reached out and put her arms around him. He hugged her back, and she understood he too was living through a loss that would change him forever.

"Shall we sit down?" asked Jackie, ushering them into the living room and towards the sofas. She sat next to Sketch and took hold of her hand connecting her to the safety of human warm.

"There's something we want to ask you Sketch," said John. "Mum had a cat. We can't take her back to Australia. She's too old and even if she survived the journey she'd be in quarantine for a year. At the moment she's being looked after by the Cat's Protection League but she needs a home. "

Sketch nodded. "Clock, that's her name right?"

"Yes, I named her when I was younger," said Martin.

"Thing is, Sketch, we wondered if you would like to have Clock?" asked John. "I think mum would like that."

Tears consisting of pride, sadness and emotional overload welled up in the lower regions of Sketch's eyes.

"I.." How could she take a cat back to the Core with her?

"Sketch would love to have Clock," said Jackie giving her a look that said everything was going to be ok.

"Ok, yes, thank you," said Sketch. "Thank you." She turned and grasped John, Martin and Sarah all at once, in a giant hug.

Chapter 19

THE FUNERAL WAS NOT until the following Monday so Sketch distracted herself over the weekend by working on her plan to stop the closure of the library. Little time remained before her planned return to the Core and she wanted to give as much as she could to the campaign to keep the vital community resource open to the public. On Sunday, Ashling and Sammy came to lunch as arranged. No one mentioned the absence of Maud but the hugs exchanged on arrival demonstrated a kindness and sympathy appreciated by Sketch. Her friends understood.

Jackie had been teaching Sketch how to cook and she held up a roast potato on her fork admiring its crispy exterior before biting through it to reveal a soft and fluffy interior.

"How are your potatoes?" she asked for the third time. Jackie and Ashling giggled.

"What potatoes?" said Ashling winking at Matt, who turned away from her look and concentrated his gaze on the plate of food in front of him.

Sketch pretended to be offended and then laughed, choking on a bit of potato she managed to inhale through her nose.

"More spuds anyone?" she asked. They all laughed, even Matt

as he shuffled peas around in the gravy.

The plates were soon cleared.

"That was delicious Sketch. Thanks so much. It's been ages since I had a roast," said Ashling.

"You're welcome," said Sketch grinning with both her mouth and her eyes.

"I'll pack some of the leftovers for you to take home Ashling," said Jackie, clearing plates from the table.

"Let me do the washing up to say thanks," said Ashling. Sammy played with Legos on the living room floor, building towers with the multi-coloured bricks. They had belonged to Matt when he was a boy.

"No, don't worry. Matt'll do it," said Jackie looking over to her grim-faced son.

"Why me?" he said, scowling.

"Oh, maybe because I cooked, Sketch helped and Ashling is a guest," said his mother in a glare indicating it would not be wise to argue back to her.

"I'll give you a hand," said Ashling.

He looked at her with scorn. "Why would I want your help?"

Sketch was taken aback at the unprovoked anger. She noticed Ashling recoil and almost shrink at the harshness of his words.

"Matt!" said Jackie. "This is not how you've been brought up. Apologise to Ashling now."

Matt stared at his mother.

"I'm your son. Why aren't you taking my side?"

"It's alright. We should be off now," said Ashling. "Come on, Sammy."

"No, please don't go, Ashling. Stay and have some tea. Matt will do the washing up," said Jackie still not looking away from her son.

Sketch stood watching, not knowing if she should try to intervene. The mood in the house had changed from a jovial family meal to an atmosphere thick with tension.

Ashling pushed back her chair, moving to sit next to Sammy who was still sticking bricks onto each other in random order.

"Sammy's enjoying it. Why don't you stay for a bit? Build a car

Life in your world

or something," said Sketch joining Ashling on the carpet. "I'll help."

Ashling shrugged but didn't get up. Jackie shoved Matt towards the kitchen ignoring his defiant behaviour.

"What was that all about?" Sketch whispered hoping she couldn't be heard through in the kitchen.

"Dunno," said Ashling. "He doesn't like me. We used to get on before Sammy came along."

"That's stupid. You being a mum is not a reason to treat you the way he just did."

"I don't want to talk about it, Sketch. It doesn't matter," said Ashling. Sketch thought Ashling looked as if it mattered more than a bit to her. She still resembled someone who had been slapped across the face.

It was quiet in the room aside from the plastic clicking sounds of the Lego construction of buildings and vehicles. Sketch thought for the first time there might be some purpose in existing as an inanimate object. Being transformed into a toy and bringing joy and learning to children would be a worthwhile existence and it probably wouldn't be too stressful. Lego bricks did get a battering, though. So, given the choice, she'd opt to be another type of toy—a cuddly teddy bear perhaps.

Jackie brought in mugs of freshly brewed tea from the kitchen and some juice for Sammy in a plastic cup Ashling brought with her from the flat.

"You know you are welcome round here anytime Ashling," said Jackie. "Even after Sketch's gone home."

Sketch began to panic but tried not to show it. In a little over two weeks she would be transported back to her own realm. She'd have to leave all this behind. She swallowed a heavy gulp of air. How would she say goodbye to them all?

"Are you alright Sketch?" asked Jackie. "You've turned a shocking shade of red."

"Yes," said Sketch taking a couple of deep breaths through her nose and imagining a stream of golden liquid sunshine filling her body. She'd read online it helped in stressful situations. "I'm just thinking about the library."

"Tell us how you are getting on with the scheme, then," said Ashling. "I'm dying to hear more about it."

After Ashling and Sammy headed home, Sketch went up to her room and scouted around the Internet for something to stop her thinking about Matt's angry outburst. Something about it made her feel uncomfortable, anxious even, despite being sure it had nothing to do with her. Matt was far from the boy she'd imagined; his nature more complex and confusing than it appeared from a distance.

Thumbing through saved websites, she remembered his blog. A recent post might shed some light on his sudden moodiness. She pointed the phone's browser towards the blog and, finding an entry from minutes before, pulled the duvet around her as if to protect her from what she might find as she read on.

It's never about me.

I'm sick of it. Anyone else feeling like this? Nothing ever seems to be about me. This afternoon we sat down to Sunday dinner. Normally, I'm at my dad's so you'd think my mum would be pleased to have me there, but for the most part I'm ignored. Everything was about S, and about her friend A, and all about this dead old lady I've never even met. I mean, it's sad she died. I'm not heartless but I didn't know her, so why should I be sad?

When I asked Mum if my girlfriend could come, too, she said there was enough people coming round. I'll be glad when S goes. Mum will have to pay some attention to me, then.

The other thing that got to me was all three of them spent the entire afternoon cooing over this toddler, A's kid. As far as I can see he doesn't do anything but crap, pee, cry and dribble food out of his mouth.

Maybe I'm being unfair. I do kind of like S. She's a bit odd, what with her obsession with sausages and the way she talks to complete strangers on the street, but she makes me laugh. She's got nothing on B but she's not so bad.

Sketch read back over the pixelated words trying to make some sense of them. Matt liked her but also thought her odd. Was she not integrating? Would this affect her chances of going back to the Core? And then, exploding from the post came the jealousy, like a fire taking hold and destroying everything in its path. Why did he not realise there was nothing to be jealous of? You didn't need both eyes to see the unlimited nature of Jackie's love for her son.

Chapter 20

SKETCH AND JACKIE huddled together outside of Our Lady Help of Christians Church, which Maud had attended.

"She helped out with homeless people as well you know?" said Sketch. Jackie rubbed her arm.

"She was a good egg. Not an actual egg of course," said Jackie. Sketch laughed then covered her mouth with her hand. "It's okay to have happy memories. Maud was loved. Look at the number of people who have come out today in this miserable, cold drizzle to pay their respects to her."

Sketch nodded. The church pews were filling up with locals of all ages.

"She lived here a long time. Think of all of those people who said hello to her on the street."

Inside the old church, those congregated greeted each other, with smiles tinged with sadness. There was a chill inside the church not broken by the ad hoc heaters situated around the sacred building. The funeral consisted of a number of hymns Sketch recognised from Songs of Praise and a moving piece from Father Andrew.

"I'd now like to ask John, Maud's son, to share some words with you," said the priest.

John rose from a front pew and walked slowly towards the front of the church. He pulled a folded A4 sheet of paper from the pocket of his black suit and cleared his throat.

"My mum…" He paused and looked around the church. Sketch saw his eyes start to fill with the silent tears, her own pushing against her resolution not to cry. "My mum was an extraordinary woman. She didn't find a cure for cancer or break any world records but she changed the world in small ways. She made me, she made me who I am today. Without Maud not only would I not exist but I wouldn't be the person who went on to have my own amazing family. Her guidance, wise words and sometimes, when deserved, reprimands put me on the path to a life far away from her but she never left me. Every day she has been in my head, running through my veins, and now she may be physically gone from us but she will stay with me and I will live for her."

He pulled a hankie from his pocket and blew his nose.

"See, she told me never to go out without a handkerchief. Since we arrived from Australia we've been met with the love of a new family, the extended family of my mum. That's all of you who've turned up today to say goodbye to her. I hope you will join me in living your life for my mum, for Maud. Thank you."

Salty tears trickled down the contours of Sketch's face. Jackie squeezed her hand and she smiled. She wasn't alone. Maud would have loved this, the parishioners, friends, and family who she loved celebrating her life and memories of her.

They couldn't go back to the house after the funeral so instead the family organised a wake in the back room of a nearby pub. The kitchen provided an array of finger foods, and tea and coffee in addition to the usual alcoholic drinks.

"I thought this would be strange," said Sketch to Jackie as she moved out of the way of someone trying to squeeze past to get to the toilet. "But it's not. Hearing all these stories about Maud is brilliant. Did you know she once took part in a pantomime?"

"It's a way for us all to say goodbye. Endings are important, you know."

"I'm still sad. There's this emptiness in me and I miss her."

"You'll always miss her but it will ease with time. My mum died when I was about your age. The memories I have of her are never far away and there are days when I get sad and angry because she's not here to share life with me. Like when Matt was born, but generally when I think of her it's with love and a hope I'm making her proud of me."

Maud's family gave her their contact details in Australia and made her promise to stay in touch. This she could do. The One would let her manipulate the odd email to them via the Internet, she would never be able to go to Australia or any of the many places around the world that filled her with wonder when she read about them. I'm lucky to have spent any time in the human world, she thought, but still.

After the funeral, she went with Jackie to pick up Clock from the cat's sanctuary. The feline creature rubbed up against her legs and purred as Sketch stroked her tortoise shell fur.

"Shame I can't take you back to the Core with me eh? But Jackie will look after you. She's promised me," she whispered to the ageing cat who purred back as if understanding her words.

Chapter 21

THE FIRST SESSION of the Silver Surfers since Maud's accident was the hardest one yet. Sketch chewed on her lip waiting for them to arrive. What sort of mood would they be in? How would they react to her idea? Her previous enthusiasm for the plan had vanished. She greeted them as they arrived and waited for them to sit down before making her announcement.

"Don't switch on the computers, yet," she said. Mr Barrington looked confused, which wasn't unusual, but so did the other members of the group.

"It's okay. I just have something to say first. It's about Maud. Well, it's sort of about Maud. I mean we all feel sad she's…she's not here with us but before she died we talked a lot about doing something different and I know she would want me to carry on." She looked around to see a few nods. "So I've invited some people to join us next week, some young people."

The group exchanged worried glances and then directed them at Sketch.

"Why Sketch? We're okay with just you," said Mr Barrington. "I'm not sure about this. Last week a gang of them teenagers nearly knocked me over, too busy shouting at each other to be bothered with an old codger like me."

"You're all going to do great. Maud was all for this idea."

The group remained unconvinced. Sketch worried they would leave.

"So why did Maud want to do this?" asked Annabel.

"Well, it started with missing her grandson. Because her family moved to Australia, she missed him growing up, all his big moments like cricket matches, birthdays, girlfriends. And even though they spoke on the phone now and then, she didn't know what to talk to him about. We thought perhaps spending some time with other teenagers might help her understand kids that age. Plus, don't you think many young people would benefit from spending time with you? You've all done so much in your lives and they're all just starting out."

Sketch stood watching the group process the idea of spending some of their time with a group of young people.

"Plus we need all of you, whatever your age, for an important job we can't tell you about just yet," she added.

"So how will it work?" asked Mrs Hale. "Will we have to share the computers with them?"

"Sort of," replied Sketch. "We're actually going to meet them all today, via the Internet." The group perked up, showing tentative interest in what Sketch had to say.

"I've got in touch with a few people I've met whilst living around here. They are all aged twenty-one and under and they've agreed to take part. Meeting online will help you find out a bit about each other before next week. It's your chance to tell them that there's more to getting older than just walking sticks and hearing aids. "

Sketch hoped meeting virtually would give them a chance to share experiences and stop being afraid of each other. They were all human beings who laughed, cried, and made mistakes. They all got scared or anxious at times, and fell in and out of love.

Some things didn't change with age.

"We're not so different inside; it just our bodies that let us down," said Annabel.

"Yes, I'm still the girl I was at eighteen, except you wouldn't want to see me on the dance floor these days," chipped in Mrs Harding-Edgar.

Sketch understood what they meant. In the Core, she'd been a pure energy free to move around in her environment untethered by the boundaries of form - neither square nor sphere, representing no physical part of the computer. Taking on the form of the cursor whilst performing her duties was the nearest she would come to having a solid form. Now, whilst loving having a body she'd chosen, she sometimes felt constrained by the formalities of her skin covered skeleton and its dense awkwardness. There were moments her mind forgot she couldn't fly and she was stuck down on the floor, unable to defy gravity with more than a small jump into the air. That must be what it felt like to grow old. To have thoughts and actions that seemed so real but in practice proved near impossible.

The plan also included getting both groups involved with stopping the proposed closure of the library but it depended on the older people grasping the basics of online communications. Sketch set up chat sessions on each of the computers before her group arrived. They'd managed to do a lot in their first couple of weeks but there were limits to their skills. It would have taken the best part of their allotted time just to go through signing up, thinking up usernames and passwords. Sketch wanted them to link up to their counterpart before her final week when she would bring them all into the library together to set up Facebook accounts for the older people.

Earlier she'd sent a message to all the young members of the project to remind them they would be corresponding with people who were new to computers. They couldn't type very fast or understand text speak. The younger participants should use the sort of language expected for job applications or school essays. Sketch hoped that, as most of them were in the sixth form or college, it wouldn't be a problem for them.

Mr Barrington had been matched with Ashling because she knew him and was aware a little bit more patience might be needed with him. Flo Foster was connected with Matt. Sketch wondered if Matt would still take part in the project after the events of the weekend and the amount of time he was spending with his girlfriend. Britney still hadn't got bored of her most recent conquest and Matt echoed her level of interest. Both Jackie and Sketch thought she was toying with him, using him until someone better came along but they couldn't say that to Matt. Sketch was pleased he had joined in today and was pinging messages back and forth to Flo. They were talking about what happened on Eastenders the previous night. Television proved an easy conversation piece but it didn't work for everyone. Annabel Bradford swore she only watched the ten o'clock news, spending the rest of her leisure time listening to Radio 4. She went to considerable effort to convince Petal to turn her dial from Radio 1 to Radio 4, swearing by The Archers as her soap opera of choice. Petal suggested some music Annabel she might like

I don't like that rap nonsense, they shout and I can't make out what they are saying.

It's not all rap. I'll bring some next week and you can tell me what you think.

The session came to a close later than planned as no one wanted to log off from their online chats. Sketch had to pry Mrs Harding Edgar away from a dialogue about sweets and chocolates and how they'd been rationed when she was a girl. Dominic had been getting a real life history lesson. Everything had gone better than she hoped but she couldn't help but be a little sad as she put everything back in its place. It had been an extraordinary afternoon and, despite some nervousness all around at the beginning, it had all come off. However, Sketch's mind was continually drawn back to Maud and how much she would have loved to take part in something like this. The old lady that had been so dear to her died before her time. This was the only way to make sure she wasn't forgotten.

"You've done an amazing job, Sketch," said Begw. "We need to take you to the pub to celebrate."

Trevor nodded from behind her.

"Thanks, but I'm not in the mood," said Sketch.

"Nonsense," said Begw. "You think that old lady of yours would be happy to know you're moping around? That's no way to celebrate her life."

"We insist," said Trevor. "Plus we need to strategise. The war is not yet won."

"Ok, but don't let me get drunk," said Sketch.

The lure of beer won and a couple of pints later Sketch was back at Jackie's ready to go to bed. She gave a cursory glance across to the computer and smiled.

"I'm coming back soon, Inco. I'm coming back."

The week continued in its regular rhythm. Tuesday turned to Friday and the weekend arrived with its promised time off. Sketch had made arrangements to go out with Jackie on a sightseeing tour of the capital.

"I'm not having you spend a month in London and only see Tufnell Park, Kentish Town and a bit of rainy South London," she said.

"As long as we don't have to go to Kennington," said Sketch laughing.

Chapter 22

JACKIE HAD PLANNED a whistle stop tour of the main attractions including Buckingham Palace, The London Eye and the Tower of London. To get around to more places she decided not to take a tourist bus but rather to take advantage of the famous Duck Tours. These tours used vehicles that had been used in the Second World War as boats to get people out of Dunkirk. It transported them around the iconic sights of the capital, with people making quacking noises as it passed. Reaching the river, the vehicle transformed itself into a little yellow boat that took them up and down a stretch of the Thames.

Because of her background, Sketch loved things that could transform. She was transfixed by the very idea of the metamorphosis that occurred when a caterpillar turned into a butterfly, so beautiful and short-lived. Her favourite book for story time remained *The Hungry Caterpillar*.

They were on their way back from Central London on the 390 bus when both Sketch and Jackie received texts on their phones.

Sammy had an accident. At Whittington. Please come.

The Whittington was a hospital in Archway, a walkable distance from Tufnell Park. The bus would take them there but because it was urgent they jumped off at Goodge Street and made the rest of the journey on the Northern Line.

Fortunately, there were no delays or planned engineering works on that section of the line. They'd tried to ring Ashling before heading underground but only got her voicemail and so had no way of knowing how serious Sammy's accident was, but after what had happened to Maud, Sketch was beside herself.

"If anything happens to him, Jackie…" Sketch began, mentally urging the tube to go faster.

"I know but I'm sure he's going to be fine."

Emerging from the tube into the cold night air, they weaved their way through the somewhat grimy streets of Archway until they reached the A&E department of the hospital. A glance around the waiting room failed to locate Ashling.

"We're looking for Ashling Peterson, well her son Sammy," Jackie told a harassed-looking receptionist behind a counter after they had been queued for ten minutes. "He was brought in earlier."

"You family?" she answered, not looking up from her computer.

"No, but were close friends and she called us."

"Take a seat, I'll get someone to come and talk to you in a bit," said the receptionist gesturing over to some rows of pale blue plastic seats.

"How long will it be?" Sketch asked Jackie after they had been waiting for ten minutes.

"I don't honestly know. They are really busy in casualty. Someone will be out soon or I'll go and ask," replied Jackie.

People came into the Accident and Emergency department broken and sick. Sitting around the injured and infectious was not pleasant. Faces displayed pain, arms clutched stomachs, and strange noises came out of people who were hurt or drunk or a combination of the two. The worst were the people who were alone and talking to themselves or people accompanying their friends who shouted at no one in particular, complaining about the NHS and its services.

Ignoring the signs on the walls banning the use of mobile phones, Sketch sent Ashling another text to let her know they were there. She must be having an awful time going through all this on her own. Another fifteen minutes passed but no one had come out to speak to them. Jackie made another attempt to find out information from the receptionist but she received the same answer. A number of people had become impatient at the long waiting times but losing their temper failed to get them any further; one man had been removed by security when he got abusive.

With no further information, they sat, waiting for a nurse or doctor to speak to them.

"It's like this on the telly, but you always think it'll be different when it's you," said Jackie. "Do you want a drink? I'm going to go and try and get a tea from the machine."

"Please, can I have a can of coke, if they've got one?" asked Sketch. Jackie went off and Sketch stood up to stretch. It wasn't comfortable sitting on the hard, plastic chairs. She would have gone for a walk but for the risk someone might take their seats while she was gone. A constant stream of traffic moved through the department despite no one being seen for ages.

Sketch was in mid-stretch, fingers reaching for her toes when she caught the eye of a nurse talking to the receptionist.

"Are you the lady asking about Sammy Peterson?" she asked.

"Yes, me and I'm with my friend Jackie. Is he okay? Where are they?" said Sketch, the words tumbling out.

"He's going to be alright but he's been taken to surgery," she said. "His parents are waiting upstairs for him to come out."

"His parents?" Ashling had always refused to tell her who Sammy's dad was. The nurse must be mistaken. It was probably just Dominic. He'd been spending a lot of time with them and it would be an easy leap for a stranger to believe he was Sammy's father.

"Can I go and see them?" asked Sketch.

"Yes, you'll need to go out, up the ramp and take the lift to the third floor. If you ask at reception, they'll show you where the family room is."

"He's in good hands," smiled the nurse as she turned back towards another emergency arrival.

Jackie arrived back with a couple of cups of tea.

"Sorry, no coke, just weak, watery tea but it's hot and wet." She handed Sketch a beige coloured plastic cup. "Was that nurse talking to you?"

"Yes, Sammy's in surgery. We can go and sit with Ashling." Sketch decided it was better not to mention "the parents" until they got there and saw who it was. It would just embarrass Dominic if he thought people were talking about him and Sammy. Sketch thought it was a real shame he wasn't Sammy's father as he got on very well with the little boy.

It was easy to navigate their way upstairs to the area of the hospital where the little boy was having his surgery. From what the nurse had told Sketch, they felt they could relax just a little. Aside from the normal risks of surgery, Sammy was in no immediate danger.

Nurses on the 3rd floor pointed them along another clinical smelling corridor, past nurses and doctors with tablets and stethoscopes.

"They're never handsome in real life like on the telly," said Jackie. "Doctors that is, not like George Clooney."

Real life was seldom as you imagined it would be, thought Sketch.

That was her experience anyway. No amount of programmes watched through the Internet could have prepared her for what it was like to have a human body or to interact with so many individual, complex people. At the beginning of her journey she couldn't have predicted she would be in a hospital waiting to see if her friend's son was going to be all right. It had been hard enough for her to imagine having human friends.

They located the family room halfway along the corridor. It was specially designed for people coming to visit who needed some time away to hide their feelings or to sit whilst their loved one was being operated on, seeing the doctor, having a bed bath or one of the other everyday routine tasks taking place on the surgical ward. Jackie opened the door and walked into the room. Sketch followed.

"Sketch!" said Ashling, turning as the door opened.

"Mum," said Matt.

"What are you doing here?" asked Jackie.

"I texted you, Ashling," said Sketch hugging her friend. "What happened? How is Sammy?"

"He fell in the park. He fell off a swing. It's my fault, I wasn't holding on properly," said Ashling. "He was on one of those swings that have the bars but I should have been watching him more."

"How is he now?" asked Jackie, turning her attention from her son who was shuffling from foot to foot.

"He's got a broken leg but it's fractured in more than one place so they have to operate," said Ashling. "They said it was lucky he didn't bump his head."

"Oh, what a relief. He'll be fine, Ashling," said Jackie. "And it's not your fault. These things happen to the best parents."

Jackie told them all about the time when Matt was very small, just crawling, and he'd fallen head first down two flights of stairs. They'd been at her parents' house where there were no stair gates and she'd turned around to get a clean nappy from a bag and he was off. She'd caught up with him just as he was taking the terrible tumble. It'd been awful but, by some miracle, nothing at all had happened to him.

"It's become a bit of a family joke. Hasn't it Matt?"

Matt grunted a nondescript response.

"You can't blame yourself is what I'm trying to say," said Jackie.

"No, it was my fault if I hadn't been…" Ashling stopped.

"Been what?" asked Sketch without thinking.

"Nothing," she said dipping her head downwards.

An awkward silence filled the room.

It's lucky we're alone, thought Sketch.

"Well, at least Sammy is going to be okay," said Sketch. "We've been so worried. You've no idea."

Ashling smiled.

"I've got some."

"Oh, yeh," said Sketch. "Sorry, that was a stupid thing for me to say."

"It's okay. It's been the worst thing ever to happen to me."

"What happened?" asked Jackie, her tone soft and encouraging.

"We were arguing and I turned around. A second, not even a minute."

Ashling squeezed her arms around her body as if trying to hold everything in.

"A second and when I turned back he'd been flung from the swing, thrown to the ground on a nearby patch of grass."

Sketch struggled for something helpful to say but the words running through her head were all clichés.

"His little body was twisted…it was horrific. There was a short delay after he hit the ground before he began to cry. I ran to him but didn't know what to do."

Ashling's eyes were cast towards the floor, fixed to the pale green hospital linoleum even as Jackie came up, putting an arm around her.

"The paramedics kept saying he was brave, a brave little boy. Said that him being conscious was a good thing, even though he was howling in pain. The worst thing was he wanted me to cuddle him but all I could do was hold his hand, stroke his head."

"He knew you were there," said Jackie. "That's the important thing."

"Doesn't feel like it's enough."

"You're a good mum, Ashling. You wouldn't be thinking like that if not."

"Where's Dominic?" asked Sketch. "I thought you were going out with him today."

"We had a fight," said Ashling.

"Really? The two of you seemed to be getting on so well."

"We were."

"So what happened?" Sketch ignoring Jackie shaking her head at her from behind Ashling.

"It was about Sammy's dad," said Ashling. "I don't want to talk about it."

Jackie tutted. "I thought Dominic was a sensible boy. I wouldn't have thought he would be jealous of someone who didn't even want to see his son."

Sketch observed Ashling as she turned away, taking it as an indication she meant what she said. Sketch walked over to her and put her arms around her. The pair sat down on the blue comfy chairs provided to ease the pain of distressed relatives.

"Well, I for one am glad he's okay," said Sketch.

The door opened and an older couple with drawn faces entered, drawing a close to the conversation. The four of them sat opposite each other waiting for Sammy to come out of surgery.

Chapter 23

IT WAS past eleven o'clock when Sketch, Jackie and Matt headed home from the hospital. With Sammy out of the operating theatre and recovering from the anaesthetic, they made their way back the short distance to Tufnell Park. Ashling remained on the ward, sitting with him as if to guard him from further dangers, but she'd insisted they all go home to rest. As her mobile phone battery had died Sketch left hers, making Ashling promise to call or text if anything happened during the night.

As soon as she got back to the house Sketch, logged onto the computer to send Dominic a message.

I don't know what happened with you and Ashling today, but I thought I should let you know that Sammy is ok. He's had surgery and will have a cast on for weeks but it's nothing life threatening. I'm sure Ashling would really like to see you tomorrow. She's going to need help once Sammy comes home.

Sketch browsed her Facebook page and the day's notifications. As she trawled her way through photo tags, comments on her Duck Tour posts, and requests to join online games, a reply from Dominic appeared in her inbox.

What do you mean? I've not seen Ashling today. I was sick this morning and didn't want to pass on my germs. What's happened to Sammy? I've been trying to text her but when she didn't reply, I just thought she'd run out of credit and I'd go round tomorrow. Now I'm confused. WTF's going on?

Sketch didn't know what to make of the message. Had she misheard Ashling when she said she'd had an argument with Dominic? She was certain her memory was accurate because she remembered Jackie disapproving of his behaviour. Plus, Ashling had not said or done anything to dismiss it, so what on the human earth was going on? She paused before replying, then let Dominic know what Ashling had told her. She missed out the bit about the argument as it was becoming clear to her that that too was a lie.

I'm sorry, Dominic. I thought you knew but don't worry about it tonight. You should call Ashling tomorrow. She's using my phone.

There was nothing else she could do and her human body was beginning to shut down for the day. She was about to close off the computer when her chat box popped up with a greeting from Harry. She smiled as her energy levels rose, wiping thoughts of tiredness from her mind as she settled back down in front of the screen.

Hi Harry. What you up to?

Just chatting to you, Sketch. I was hoping to catch you earlier.

I was out sightseeing. Just like a tourist and then my friend's son had an accident, so we've been at the hospital.

Oh no, is he okay?

Yeh, he's good. He's going to be fine but it was a bit scary.

So you've been helping people again? I reckon you're really kind, like an angel.

*I'm not that kind, really. *blushes**

You look cute when you blush.

Sketch responded with haste, trying to match sentence by sentence the level of flirtation transmitted in Harry's messages. When things got too heated she directed the conversation back to the events of Sketch's day. She still couldn't get her head around Ashling's comments about Dominic and their alleged fight.

It just doesn't make sense. Why would she say that if it wasn't true?

Sometimes people make things up because it's easier.

What do you mean?

I should think Ashling told you that cos she didn't want to tell you what really happened. Maybe she's embarrassed.

I just don't get what she's got to be embarrassed about.

It sounds like she had a huge argument with someone and it wasn't Dominic.

She said goodbye to Harry leaving a couple of kisses on her final chat message and shut down the computer. There was an answer to her question hiding in the back of her mind but Sketch didn't want to think about it, not yet.

Sketch slept much later than was usual for a Sunday, waking at eleven o'clock when her dreams were interrupted by Jackie bringing in a cup of tea. She blinked and attempted to hide her head underneath the duvet. It felt harder to wake up than during the week when her alarm went off at seven.

"Uumrggh, thanks," she said, pulling a face as Jackie opened the curtains.

"Ashling rang," said Jackie.

Sketch sat up and took a sip from the mug of builders' strength tea.

"Yeh? Is everything okay? Is Sammy all right?" Tea somehow managed to revive her in a way nothing else could.

"Don't panic, everything is fine. They're going to keep Sammy in for another day. Just to make sure there are no complications. Should be home tomorrow morning," said Jackie.

"That's brilliant news. Can we go and see them today?" asked Sketch.

"Yes, I said we'd come down for lunchtime, see Sammy and then we can take Ashling down to the food court and buy her a proper meal."

"Good idea," said Sketch. "I hear the food there is really good."

Jackie laughed. Sketch could be convinced to do almost anything as long as there was food involved.

"I bet she's not eaten properly since this happened."

Sketch pulled on a pair of jeans and selected a fluffy purple jumper. She accessorised it with a chunky black bead necklace and matching ear-rings. Looking pretty made her feel less tired and that was important today. She needed all her energy for the visit to the hospital. You have to be cheery when you are visiting the sick, positivity being a crucial weapon in the battle of recovery. She'd gleaned this good advice from a website on healthcare Jackie had been browsing one day. There were other challenges the day was likely to bring, and this was just her way of making sure she was on top form and prepared for whatever was thrown at her. After adding some makeup to her clothing mask, she smiled at her reflection in the mirror, high fived herself and headed downstairs.

"Hi, Sketch," said Matt as they passed on the stairs down to the kitchen and living room.

"Hi, Matt. We're off to the hospital in a mo to see Ashling and Sammy. You coming?" asked Sketch.

"Er, no. I'm going to see Britney," said Matt looking away from her pointed gaze.

"Any messages then?"

"No, not really. Just say I'm glad Sam's okay." Matt dashed up the final set of stairs, grabbed his winter coat and ran out of the house. Sketch sighed as she heard the front door slam behind him. She knew she was right, her online chat with Harry had confirmed her suspicions about the father of Ashling's baby. But she didn't want to think about it right now so pushed it all to the back of her mind and headed to the living room to get Jackie.

Chapter 24

WHEN THEY ARRIVED at the hospital, Sammy was sitting up in bed wriggling around but constrained by a purple plaster cast encasing his leg.

"That's just waiting to be written on," said Jackie after checking everything was okay with the pair.

"They should give away packs of pens with each cast," said Ashling. She looked tired but alongside the effects of lack of sleep her face displayed visible signs of relief.

It must have been traumatic for her, thought Sketch. The line between life and death appeared sharper to her since losing Maud. She could understand a little of the fear Ashling must have experienced.

Sketch and Jackie both signed the cast with an eyeliner Sketch kept for make up emergencies in her handbag. To add some fun to the cast they drew happy faces on it making Sammy giggle.

"Arms, too?" he said holding out both his arms for the same smiley face treatment as his leg cast. Everyone laughed and Sketch instinctively ruffled his short ginger hair.

"You girls go off and get some lunch. I'll sit and keep Sammy company," said Jackie.

"If you're sure," said Ashling. "I don't really want to leave him but now that you mention it, I'm starving."

"We insist," said Sketch taking her by the arm and leading her off towards the lift.

The food court at the Whittington had a good range of eating and drinking options. Tempting though a full English breakfast for lunch was, the two friends opted for the healthier food choice and had a plate of boiled new potatoes, salmon and green veg each. Sketch watched Ashling attack the plate of food, shovelling forkful after forkful into her mouth. Sketch, in contrast, nibbled at her potatoes.

"You alright Sketch?" Ashling asked.

"Just thinking." She pushed some soggy broccoli around the white canteen standard plate.

"Careful now, that'll do you damage," said Ashling, laughing at her own bad attempt at humour.

"Thing is, Ash, that it doesn't make sense." Sketch looked up from her food and across to her friend.

"What?"

"The thing you said about having an argument with Dominic."

Ashling's face drained of colour.

"I don't know what you mean."

"How could you have an argument with him when he says he didn't speak to you all day? Why are you lying to me?"

"I don't know," she put her hands through her hair. "I didn't know what else to do. I thought…I don't know what I thought."

"So who was there?" asked Sketch. She was uncomfortable at the distress she was causing Ashling but it was too late to put the stop what was about to happen. "Was it Matt?"

Ashling nodded. "He won't listen. I've tried to tell him before but he just won't listen."

The pair sat there not speaking, not eating, not looking at one another.

"He's Sammy's dad," said Ashling, exhaling the words as if they were captives she'd been trying to liberate for a long time.

"I'd kind of guessed," said Sketch leaning over and touching her friend's hand in much the same way as Maud had once done to her sitting in a cafe. "But I don't get why he's not been helping you and why Jackie doesn't know."

"I never told anyone. When I eventually did summon up the courage to talk to him, he refused to listen. According to Matt I'd been sleeping with half the boys in the school, but there was only him."

Sketch sat listening, trying to take in Ashling's words.

"After a while I gave up. Decided we'd be better off on our own, me and Sammy, that is."

Realising this was going to take a little longer, Sketch went for coffees and cake. This was a moment requiring the comfort of cake. Ashling told her how she'd had a crush on Matt for over a year and how one night at a party, not unlike Rochelle's they'd got together.

"I thought all my Christmases had come at once," said Ashling. "Thing was, Matt didn't want anything serious. In fact, all he wanted was a quick shag."

Sketch was appalled. Any remaining attraction she had to Matt had been totally blown away by Ashling's revelations. And Jackie, this would devastate Jackie.

"It was a couple of months before I realised I was pregnant and by then he wouldn't even speak to me. I was invisible. Not cool enough for him."

"What about your parents?"

Ashling described how her mum and dad had insisted on knowing the father of the child but she refused to tell them. They had been more bothered about what people would think about them than helping her through the pregnancy and the birth of her baby.

"They're rather old-fashioned. I'm sure not all parents are like that these days. I swear I'll never be the same with my Sammy," she said.

"So what happened yesterday in the park?" asked Sketch beginning to piece the bits of the jigsaw together in her head.

"After what happened at dinner last week I decided things

needed to change," said Ashling. "I loved being there, being part of a family until Matt went and threw all his toys out of the pram."

Sketch nodded for Ashling to continue.

"I rang him and asked him to meet me in the park. He said no, so I told him I would go round and see his mum if he didn't."

It had worked. Matt had met Ashling and Sammy at the swings.

"I chose the park because it's neutral territory. Or I thought it was. Perhaps a children's playground was the wrong choice. He went mad. Shouting at me, going on that I was trying to trap him and that he wasn't Sammy's dad. All the kids playing, shouting loudly and running around without a care in the world seemed to freak him out even more."

"Then, as we were both sniping at each other, it happened. He fell, Sammy fell from the swing," said Ashling, tears falling down her face. Sketch recognised them as the hot, silent tears she had shed when Maud had died.

"But he came to the hospital," said Sketch, handing Ashling a tissue.

"Yeh, it was as if it snapped him out of it. He was so worried about Sammy."

"It didn't last very long," said Sketch trying not to judge Matt too harshly but finding herself further disappointed in what she was discovering about him.

"I just don't care much anymore. I've got Sammy and that's all that matters." Ashling wiped her face with a paper napkin.

"But what about Jackie?"

The question hung in the air. Sketch knew she couldn't tell Jackie. It wasn't her secret to part with but she was also certain life would be better for all of them if Jackie knew she had become a granny.

"That's up to Matt," said Ashling. "I'm not going to march in and make a big announcement."

Chapter 25

MONDAY MORNING SAW Sketch back in the library, filling up on tea and biscuits with Begw and Trevor. With no one else to talk to about it, she found herself spilling the beans about the dramatic events of the weekend including Ashling's confession.

"Really? It's better than telly your life," said Trevor before attempting to beat the world record of how many hobnobs you could have in your mouth at the same time.

"Does the name hobnobs have anything to do with your sudden bid for fame?" asked Begw whipping out her smartphone to snap a photo of the epic biscuit record fair to post on online.

"We'll be one down for story time this week then?" asked Begw thinking once again about falling user numbers and the on-going threat of closure.

"This week, at least. It's hard for them to get around and the pushchair doesn't accommodate the giant leg cast," said Sketch.

"There must be something they can do," said Trevor. "They can't stay in for weeks until the cast comes off."

"Dominic is going to pick up another buggy later. His neighbour has one she doesn't need anymore. But Ashling said they won't make it for story time. She's promised they'll do their best for tomorrow," said Sketch.

Tomorrow was the final session with the Silver Surfers group, the second part of Sketch's intergenerational project and a chance for her to play a part in saving the library before she departed. A cute, little boy with his leg in plaster was going to get a lot of attention from the members of the group. She was worried about how Matt would react if Ashling turned up, even without Sammy. She was going to have to make an effort to speak with him about this before tomorrow.

Sketch sent Matt a text to find out whether he would be in this evening, not wanting to miss him because he was out with Britney. This time his girlfriend would have to wait, she thought. Matt seemed reluctant to meet with her in his reply but Sketch insisted.

Matt asked if they could meet in one of the cafes on Fortess Road and was sitting waiting when Sketch arrived.

"Hi, do you want a drink?" asked Sketch.

Matt pointed towards the mug he was holding and shook his head. Sketch ordered and then sat down at the table opposite him.

"Did you have a good day?" she asked.

"Cut the crap Sketch. That's not why you wanted to meet me is it?" Matt sounded irritated, nervous and the tone of his voice mean.

"No, I wanted to talk about Ashling," she paused. "And Sammy."

"It's really none of your business. Just leave it alone."

"Ashling is my friend and you are, too. And it seems to me you're missing out on the life of your son because you are scared," she said. No point holding back now.

"I don't even know if he's mine."

"He's yours."

They stared at each other, iris to iris in standoff position.

Sketch hadn't finished yet. She took a deep, inner breath before continuing.

"However it happened, he's your son and not only do you have a responsibility to look after him, not only that but you are missing him grow up, and him having a family."

"But..."

"No, let me finish," said Sketch, refusing to let him interrupt. "I'm not for a minute suggesting that you move in with them but Sammy deserves to have a dad and a granny."

"Mum would kill me," said Matt.

"Okay, so at first she's going to be shocked but she likes Ashling and Sammy, she'll come round."

"I can't tell her," said Matt ripping up a paper serviette into odd shaped pieces.

"What about your dad? Can you tell him?"

"Jesus, no. He's worse than mum. I'd be better off without him," said Matt.

Sketch hadn't met Matt's dad and he'd not been to stay with his dad during the time she'd been with him, but it seemed to her what was holding Matt back was the fear he wouldn't be good enough, and that Sammy would end up with a life lacking. It was as if Matt believed Sammy didn't need him or any father figure.

"You'd have plenty of help you know. And Sammy wouldn't really know any different as you've never lived there," said Sketch.

"Sketch, I'm seventeen. In a year and a half, I'll be at university. I can't do that if I've got a kid to look after," said Matt.

"And what about Ashling? Don't you think she'd like to be at school with no worries in the world?" Sketch was annoyed at Matt's selfish attitude.

"I don't know what to say, Sketch. You want me to be something I'm not. I'm just a kid," argued Matt.

"And so is Ashling," fired back Sketch. She sighed, put some money down on the table to pay for her drink and stormed out of the café.

Why wouldn't Matt listen? Nothing she said made a dent in his armour. It was so frustrating. Why should Ashling have to struggle alone when there was a ready-made support network just around the corner?

The day of the final Silver Surfers session arrived. Sketch's argument with Matt left her wanting her own company and she spent most of the evening in her room thinking over what had happened. Awakening the next morning, her negative thoughts and niggles were pushed to a storage area of her brain, leaving space for her to be excited about the day ahead.

She was surprised to find that her nerves were back and amidst the excitement was a jittery, sensation of butterflies fluttering around in her stomach. Although the older people had met their younger counterparts online, they hadn't yet seen each other face-to-face. There was still a chance they wouldn't get on.

"Hello, Sketch," said Mr Barrington ambling across the library in high-waisted trousers and brown thick-rimmed glasses. He resembled a character in a film about life in the 1950s. "Is it computers today?"

"Hello Mr Barrington. Yes, it is," she replied, smiling, glad he had remembered. "You're just on time. Have a sticker and write your name on it."

As the members of the class and their counterparts came in, they followed Mr Barrington's lead, filling in their names on the white stickers Sketch had laid out for them. They stood around sneaking glimpses at each other, fiddling with bags, coats and phones, leaving Sketch to make the initial introductions. After some sharing of names and favourite books, the noise level rose to above the acceptable norm for a library, making it difficult for Sketch to get their attention.

"Right. Trevor is going to take some photos of you all for your profiles. Who wants to go first?" asked Sketch.

Annabel Bradford fumbled in her handbag, pulling out a hairbrush and a pasta pink lipstick.

"Oh, that's a good idea," said Flo following suit.

The group was keen to look their best and coerced Trevor into taking more than one shot.

"Do you like this one, Mr Barrington," he asked.

"Is that me? I look pretty dapper, don't I?"

Sketch suppressed a giggle. Trevor had grumbled when asked to

Life in your world

play photographer but from the way he interacted with the group members he appeared to be in his element.

"You look just like a model, Mrs Harding-Edgar," said Rochelle.

As the older people were being captured in pixels one by one, the young people began to help them to set up the new Facebook profiles.

"What kind of music do you like then?"

"I'm a fan of Sinatra and I quite like them Spice Girls," said one of the ladies.

There were more surprises as the generations found they had more in common than they'd imagined.

"You've got original Beatles on vinyl?" asked Dominic. He was a keen buyer of vinyl but could never dream of having a collection to rival Mr Moore's.

"From Help to the White Album. Not only that but back in the 1960s I worked on the ships and John Lennon's car was on our boat. When we got to shore I met him and he took us for a drink. Nice chap, not cocky at all," said Mr Moore.

Sketch laughed as she observed a pair at a computer discussing slang and young language. They each had their own. The older man recalling the speech of his formative years.

Facebook profiles were taking shape on computer screens as the pairs worked together, adding each other as friends. The Silver Surfers were thrilled to be exploring this new technology, although still a little cautious.

"What happens if I press the wrong thing and all this disappears? I don't want to break it," said Mr Moore.

"Nah, it's nearly impossible to get rid of your Facebook profile," said Dominic.

"Can we come back next week?" asked Rochelle.

Sketch's face lit up.

"Well, I won't be here and the course is over but we'd really like you to come back, in fact we are going to need your help."

Chapter 26

TOWARDS THE END of the session, Begw caught Sketch's eye and signalled that it was time. Having brought everyone together under the pretence of completing the set up of their Facebook accounts, the pair would now reveal the real purpose of the day.

"Alright, everyone," said Begw, waiting until the Silver Surfers and their young counterparts turned away from their monitors, the last few poking the others to get their attention.

"What I'm about to tell you could get me into big trouble so it's important that you don't mention to anyone that I told you."

"Ohhh, sounds intriguing. Are you one of them spies like off the telly?" said Mr Barrington, his bushy eyebrows protruding upward from his forehead.

The ladies in the group began nudging each other and whispers of "spy" began to circulate. As amusing as the idea of working for MI5 was, Begw kept a straight face and carried on.

"If I was I couldn't tell you, but what I'm going to say is important. It affects all of us here today.

"You all know how the government has been cutting back on everything. Well, the upshot of it all is the council doesn't have enough money to run all the services they have so they want to close the library."

Sketch surveyed the room. Faces had taken on dazed expressions, some shocked, others surprised and more than one mouth gaped open.

"But can't you do anything Begw," asked Ashling pulling Sammy closer to her.

"I can't cos I work for the council, don't I?"

"Surely there's something you can do. A protest or something?" said Annabel Bradford.

"I can't do anything because I work for the council," repeated Begw. "But none of you work for the council. Even Sketch here doesn't work for the council. She's a volunteer."

"What are you saying?" asked Dominic.

"She's saying," said Sketch standing up before the group, "that we can try and stop the library being closed. If it's important to you, that is."

The murmuring amongst the group recommenced.

"But what can we do?" asked Ashling. "We're just ordinary people. No one is going to listen to us."

Mr Barrington stood up, repositioned his tie and cleared his throat.

"I'll have you know that ordinary people have been changing the world for as long as I can remember." Giggles escaped from some of the younger members of the group.

"Oh, you know what I mean," he said.

"He's right," chipped in Annabel. "There's plenty who'll listen if we kick up enough fuss. I'll get the WI involved and Mrs Brady who lives down the road from me has a son who works for the BBC. Get some cameras down here and we'll get them bods at the council to listen."

The mood in the room began to change from shock to determination and a little excitement that something out of the ordinary was about to happen.

"We can tweet on that Facebook thingy," said Flo.

"On Twitter, not Facebook. Have you learnt nothing?" asked

Mr Moore. "Begw, the library can't close. We all depend on it. What do we do?"

Begw leant over and put her arm around Sketch.

"I'm going to leave you in the very capable hands of young Sketch. Given my job I can know nothing about what you are planning." She winked, patted Sketch on the shoulder and headed off to the staff room for a *panad*.

"First things first," said Sketch addressing the room. "We need to make a plan. If you've got time, I'd like you to spend half an hour doing some research about other libraries that have been under threat and what they did."

There was no disagreement about what needed to be done. The group turned back to their computers and got stuck into the task of sourcing ideas for campaigning against the closure. The urgency and focus of their task dissolved many of the perceived differences between the generations, leaving them more relaxed in each others' company. They worked steadily for the next hour, making notes, bookmarking information, and sharing ideas.

"Sorry, guys," said Sketch. "I hate to stop you but it's closing time." Watches, phones and computer screens were checked to verify the time. "But if you can come back tomorrow we can decide the best action to take."

Sketch noticed levels of tension between Matt and Ashling had been raised in the library that day. The session went by without a word exchanged between the pair. They are so stubborn, thought Sketch. Matt seemed still to be in denial about being a father, the sight of Sammy in the library that afternoon making it ever more real. If she'd not come to the human realm and met Ashling perhaps nothing would have happened but she wasn't sure her interventions brought any improvement to the situation. Matt's behaviour towards Sketch had cooled and Ashling still believed Sammy would be better off not knowing him.

Sketch saw it as her responsibility to at least attempt to do something about the situation before she returned to the Core. Something that would make life easier for Ashling. It was too convenient for Matt to forget he'd played a key role in the appearance of the little boy in the world, too easy to carry on hoping it would all settle down again once Sketch left, with no reason for Sammy and his mum to keep turning up in his life as if it was the norm.

Deciding to try to talk to him again, Sketch grabbed her coat and snuck out of the library, following a short way behind him as he walked down the road towards home.

Up ahead, Matt pulled his coat tightly around him. The temperature had dropped now that it was dark and the late afternoon air took on a chill that seeped through layers of clothing until it penetrated your bones. The winter had a way of cancelling out the day prematurely despite the challenge of street lights and the festive illuminations popping up in shops and local roads.

The streets were busy with people hurrying home to lock themselves into the warmth of their houses for the night and Sketch was weaving her way between them, careful not to get too close to Matt when he walked straight into an oncoming pushchair.

"Oi, look where you are going," he said. Sketch edged close enough to see his mouth open and close quickly as he came level with Ashling.

"Me? Look where I'm going? You were the one who walked into us. I mean, a pushchair with a small kid in it is pretty easy to see, especially when he's your son."

The two stood staring at each other. Sketch wondered whether she should reveal herself. Both of their faces tensed up and determined.

"Why do you keep saying that?" said Matt

"What? Calling Sammy your son? Because he is. I didn't sleep with anyone else. I've never slept with anyone else. He's yours Matt, and you can say what you like but that's just not going to change."

"But I can't be a father."

"You *are* a father, fact," shouted Ashling.

Sketch wanted to reach out to her. From her viewpoint behind a man distributing copies of the Evening Standard, she could see the tears pooling in Ashling's grey eyes. Why couldn't Matt just admit the truth?

"It's not like I'm asking you for money or even to look after him."

"What do you want from me Ashling?" said Matt. Both of them appeared oblivious to the end of the day commuters squeezing their way around them in an attempt to get to the entrance of the tube station.

"You know what I want. Why do I have to spell it out for you? It's not like you're stupid with all your GCSEs."

A low vibration came from the inside pocket of Sketch's coat reminding her she'd forgotten about meeting Begw and Trevor for drinks. A pre-leaving do leaving do. The Welsh knew how to do things in style, Begw claimed.

Where are you? We're waiting.

On my way.

Shoving her mobile into her bag she turned back to see Ashling storm off with Sammy in the pushchair and Matt walking off a side road.

Chapter 27

SKETCH DISCOVERED she was much better at consuming alcohol now she'd had some practice, and found her limits. She remained surprised at how quickly her tolerance to alcoholic drinks had expanded but she'd not yet veered into the domain of binge drinking and so when at nine thirty-one pm she arrived back at the house she was confident of being a little tipsy and no more. On opening the door, she heard an unfamiliar sound. Jackie was shouting.

"How the hell could you have been so stupid? Did you think I wouldn't find out? I had to hear it from Margie Simmons on Facebook!"

Sketch wasn't sure if she should go down to the kitchen so paused a little on the stairway. She decided to listen for a little while longer to see if it was safe to proceed.

"Facebook. For the whole bloody world to see."

Matt, who Sketch assumed was the recipient of this rage, didn't say a word. Not that there was much chance of anyone cutting into Jackie's torrent of furious words.

"I'm so angry with you. I thought I brought you up better than this. Why did you not tell me? Why?" she shouted.

There was a pause. Sketch imagined Jackie wringing her hands through her hair in frustration. Her face turning a distinctive colour of red akin to that of a beetroot. Sketch struggled to hear Matt's words as he began to mumble his response.

"Cos I thought you be angry," he said. "And you are."

"Angry? Of course I'd be angry but I would have calmed down. I could have helped you. I'm supposed to help you."

Jackie's sigh was audible from Sketch's position on the landing and she judged the break in the shouting a good time to let it be known she'd arrived back from the pub.

She decided tipsy and cheerful was the wrong way to blunder down the stairs so instead put on her most serious face and tiptoed tentatively down towards the kitchen. Or she did until the alcohol took over and she lost her footing. She slid down, grappling around with her arms for a railing instead grabbing hold of a picture of some splodges in a wooden frame. It wasn't enough to keep her from rolling all the way to the bottom of the staircase. As she sat confused in a heap at the bottom of the stairs Sketch gagged and then vomited the contents of her stomach onto her trousers and the floor around her.

"I'm sorry, I'm sorry. Why are you shouting at Matt? Is it because he had a baby?"

The adverse effects of the alcohol she'd drunk earlier made her giddy. The taste of sick stuck to the hairs of her nostrils and blood pumped around her body faster than usual as she cringed, realising she'd disclosed Ashling's secret, ruined the carpet and would be waking up the next morning with another hangover.

Jackie and Matt busied themselves cleaning up Sketch and anywhere she'd managed to soil with her alcoholic spew, before bundling her off to bed with a bottle of flat coca cola and a pink plastic bucket.

"Sip on it, it will rehydrate you. Matt and I have something we need to discuss. Sleep well, Sketch," said Jackie helping her up to her room to avoid another tumbling incident.

❄

Life in your world

AS LIGHT SNEAKED in through the curtains of Sketch's window she held her face between both hands, resisting the day's arrival. Her skull ached, as if a small rodent had crawled inside of her head, settled in a hollow just above her eyes and was knocking on her skull shouting, "Let me out. Let me out."

From her mouth emitted a sound reflecting her pain, half groan, half squeal. *Not another hangover*, she thought before beginning to put together the fragments of mangled memories from the night before. One by one, they dropped like Tetris blocks into place in her mind. Coming in, standing on the landing, Jackie and Matt arguing, shouting and a tumble down the stairs, apparently in slow motion. Just a hangover sounded much better.

Sketch's last day in the house fell on a Saturday. The plan was to return to the computer late at night, when Matt had gone out or to bed. Jackie and Sketch had hatched a cover story about Sketch being picked up by a relative from home.

Emerging from her room, Sketch stood in the hall and listened to the quiet of the house, through which she heard the predictable ticking of a clock, the creaking of the building's frame. She could also smell the aroma of Jackie's organic, fair-trade coffee calling upon her nostrils. She squeezed her eyes together trying to quash the throbbing pain and headed towards the kitchen. Before her feet made it to the second step the familiar chime of the doorbell caused her to turn around.

"Dominic, hi," she said opening the door.

"Hi Sketch, how you doing?"

Sketch grimaced and pointed towards her head. She skipped the bit about falling down the stairs under the influence of a few too many.

"Oh, I know that feeling," he grinned. "Come on, I hear there's some decent coffee on offer. Cup of tea and a paracetamol and you'll be fine in no time."

"Alright, but we've all got to get to the library soon. They'll be thinking we've given up on them."

Sketch followed Dominic down to the kitchen, reassured that if she fell again he would cushion her fall. To her surprise, they were met by hellos from not just Jackie but also from Matt, Ashling and Sammy.

Jackie gestured to Sketch and Dominic to get a coffee and sit down with them at the kitchen table.

"How are you feeling, Sketch? That's was a fair tumble down the stairs last night," said Jackie.

"Okay," replied Sketch. "But my head is banging."

"Any dizziness? We need to make sure you have no concussion."

"No, I'm fine. Why's everyone here?" asked Sketch.

Jackie smiled.

"I thought, given that little Sammy here is part of the family, we should all sit down and work out how we go forward with this."

Sketch grinned, but remembering how angry Jackie had been the night before, allowed the muscles around her mouth to descend.

"I'm sorry, I knew. You know I knew but I couldn't tell you."

Jackie patted her hand. "It's fine. You were keeping Ashling's secret like a good friend would but we all know now and I'm thrilled to have a grandson."

Over a large breakfast and what seemed like endless cups of tea, the friends and family discussed Sammy and how they could help to give him the best childhood.

"What we all want is for Sammy to have everything he needs. To be safe and loved," said Jackie. "I've lived more years than you and things will get tough."

Matt groaned. "Here she goes."

Jackie shot him a look.

"Sorry Mum. Just joking."

"We're not quite back on jesting terms yet." She looked around at the others assembled round the table. "It seems to me Sammy will have support from both parents and his grandparents, if that's alright with you, Ashling?"

Ashling touched cheeks with Sammy who she'd sat on her lap. "What do you think? Would you like a grannie and daddy?"

Sammy giggled and picked up a red plastic T-Rex, plonking it into the sugar bowl. He roared loudly.

"I think that's a yes in dinosaur," said Ashling. Her face

reddened. "There's someone else I'd like to help, too. Two people in fact."

"Who's that?" asked Sketch distracted from her urge to begin a fake dinosaur fight with Sammy's T-Rex.

"You silly. You and Dominic."

"Really?" Sketch and Dominic responded in unison.

"Of course. I know you're leaving but we can stay in touch, can't we?" said Ashling, focusing on Sketch.

Sketch sprang from her chair and over to Ashling, hugging her tightly.

"Nothing, could stop me."

"Dominic, okay with you? And Matt, with you?" Both boys nodded and shook hands awkwardly.

The clock on the kitchen wall caught Sketch's attention.

"Should we be going? I don't want to be late for library meeting."

"We're okay for time," said Jackie. "There's something else I wanted to raise." She turned to Ashling. "We've had a talk, Matt and I and we think with Sketch leaving, you and Sammy should move into the house."

"We couldn't. It's fine we've got the flat and it's not very far. You can come round all the time," argued Ashling.

"But, and I'm not trying to be offensive here Ashling, your flat is damp and cold. That's not your fault but if you stay here it will be better for both you and Sammy's health," said Jackie.

Sketch knew Jackie well enough to realise she was determined to get her way.

"We'll be able to help you with Sammy and you would be able to go back to school and do your A-Levels."

The thought of regaining the chance of an education, combined with a house that didn't smell of mould began to sway Ashling to Jackie's proposal.

"I like here," said Sammy making everyone giggle. Matt ruffled his son's hair, pulled his fingers away and then returning them with more confidence.

Emotions filled Sketch, creeping through her veins, around her organs and across the synaptic gaps in her brain. She experienced a combination of pride, excitement and apprehension about her forthcoming return to the Core. Her human entanglements would vanish. The threads of her life and those around her seemed woven into a picture of happiness, but what she knew now was it took very little to unravel such a tableau.

"Sketch," said Matt. "Sketch," his voice becoming louder at the second attempt to get her attention.

She jolted upwards in her seat. "Sorry, must have been daydreaming. What were you saying?"

Jackie walked over to the fridge and brought forth a large gooey chocolate cake. She fiddled with some matches, lighting ten stripy pink candles.

"Sketch, we've loved having you here and hope you'll stay in touch with us."

Sketch tried to hold in a further tangled bundle of emotions but didn't do a very good job of it. The pink glow of embarrassment spilled out across her cheeks, a watery swell of happy teardrops formed in her eyes and a smile of love began to form from her mouth.

"I'm going to miss you all so much."

❄

THE MONTH HAD PASSED TOO QUICKLY, as if time were a slab of cheese someone had been nibbling away, chomping on every minute and second until only crumbs remained. Sketch wanted to savour them, take everything in through her human senses so as not to forget what she'd learnt. The joy, exhilaration, and tenderness of their world, and its anger, shame, fear and sadness, the things that made her friends human.

They gathered around and took their turn to hug her and pass on their own personal messages of departure before leaving for the library, after which they would go their separate ways. She was most touched by Matt.

"Without you I'd still be angry and I wouldn't have Sammy," he mumbled, hair dipping over his eyes. She hugged him back amused she had once had a crush on him. It was best not to mention that.

"You're all amazing. I so wish I could stay around and help to save the library but my... my family needs me, too," said Sketch.

"Talking of which, we'd best get over there. They'll think we've been run over by a bus," said Dominic.

Everyone stared at Dominic whose choice of words reminded them all of the loss of Maud.

"Oh God. Sorry. I meant…I didn't mean," he sputtered awkwardly.

"Last one out the door's a loser," said Matt. There was a scramble for everyone to grab coats, scarves, hats, lace up shoes and get up the stairs.

Chapter 28

THE LIBRARY WAS abuzz with voices. Mr Moore had appointed himself as de facto team leader, declaring his years at sea were good training for the discipline needed to spearhead a campaign to save the library.

"Hello, better late than never," he said seeing the four stragglers enter through the door. "We've put all our ideas and information on post-its and added them to flip charts showing either online, that's the Internet stuff," he added in case of doubt. "Or the real world, the bit without computers."

Sketch approached the wall, reading the selection of campaign ideas detailed on the multi-coloured paper squares.

"Councils have to provide libraries, it's the law. Does anyone know a lawyer?" she began to read them aloud.

"Politicians might help. Contact MP and councillors by letter and email."

"Have a sit-in/book-in."

"Start up a Facebook group."

"Lock ourselves in the library and refuse to move. Call the TV people."

"Make YouTube videos."

"We could run the library ourselves but what about Begw and Trevor?"

"Get a petition together."

"March on the council."

"Dress up as books and barricade the road."

"Give leaflets out in all the local shops."

"There's so many of them," she said turning to her friends. "How do we decide what to do, Mr Moore?" she asked.

"Well, we thought we'd divide them up. Some of us are going to make a video, go out on the streets and ask the people what they love about the library. Others are going to work on a petition. And then we are planning a big sit-in in a week's time," he replied.

"Fantastic," said Sketch trying to sound excited but feeling a little lacklustre.

"Can you help us with the online campaign? Getting people involved and telling them about the sit-in?"

"Well, yes, but only today. I'm not here after today."

"We know," said Mr Barrington, "but there's still plenty of time to sort out Facebook and maybe Twitter too."

"Of course there is," she beamed. Eyes turned towards her, all of them. She looked around her to see what they were staring at.

"Err, Sketch…" Mr Moore stopped and looked at the others as if seeking help. In return, he received smiles of encouragement but when no one took over or put the words into his mouth he thrust his hand from behind his back with a beautiful bunch of flowers in it.

"Gosh," said Sketch. "I don't know what to say."

"Neither did Mr B," said Dominic, making everyone laugh.

Their conversations continued as they exited the library, making their way onto Kentish Town Road and its frenzy of people. Sketch hugged herself, both arms tight around her tiny body. She felt conflicted, her plan inspired by Maud was falling into place but joy she thought she would be experiencing at this moment was absent. Maud wasn't there. It was all ending and nothing she'd done felt like enough, despite reassurances from Jackie that the One had authorised her return to the Core.

With her emotions tangled like a ball of wool left in a basket with a kitten, Sketch wandered back across the library to the staff room. On the side, next to the kettle was a gift-wrapped package and a card with her name written on the envelope in large, black swirly writing. She looked around, moved over and began opening the present, setting aside the card on the work surface she removed the crunchy sounding tissue paper, to reveal a pint glass that looked suspiciously like it had been liberated from the Junction Tavern. The card confirmed this with a message in Welsh that translated as "This is to remind you of time spent in North London (and the pub). We'll miss you and your sausages. Love from Begw and Trevor."

The gift broke through Sketch's fog of sadness, returning a smile to her face as Begw and Trevor popped their heads through the doorway.

"Alright?" asked the Library Manager. "We've locked up and thought we'd all just pop to the Pineapple for a pint. You've not been there yet and you can't leave North London without going to The Pineapple."

Not giving her a chance to protest the pair whisked her off for a final drink at their favourite local pub.

Sketch arrived back to a quiet house. Matt had left earlier to go to his dad's. She found Jackie sitting on the edge of the sofa, the computer booted up.

"Hi."

"Hi."

The pair looked at each other. Tears began to fight for a place in the corner of Sketch's eye but she fought them off. Jackie held out her arms.

"Come here hon."

Folded up in Jackie's arms Sketched breathed in her scent, the fragrance of her shampoo, and her warmth. She let her eyes take in the tones and colours of the room, imprinting them in her mind, before she began the reverse transformation which would return her to her normal existence as an energy in the monochromatic Core of the computer. She pulled away from Jackie, sniffing.

"I don't know what to say. Your world is full of hurdles, emotions, complexities. There's still much for me to learn, so many things to experience. You've all been so kind to me, especially you." She paused, searching for the right words. "I don't want to go."

Jackie took the young woman's hands.

"You'll never know how much difference you have made to our lives," she smiled. "Not that I'll miss your habit of being sick after a few drinks."

"But it was only twice and last night…" protested Sketch.

"I'm kidding. In truth, I'll feel so much better knowing that it's you inside the computer. My lovely, bubbly Sketch with her funky white hair making everything right." They laughed.

Experiencing the physicality of her body, the smells of the world, the incredible visions her eyes allowed her, made it harder to leave behind everything she'd built in the past few weeks. How could it all disappear from her grasp?

"Not long now," said Jackie fidgeting with a coffee coaster. Sketch nodded. Waiting for anything seemed to be the worst part.

At the appointed time, Jackie inserted the device into the computer's USB port. The pulse of the One began to translate into words on the screen in front of them.

- Hello Sketch. It's time for your return. I hope this time has given you a chance to learn about why what you do inside the computer is very important.

Sketch looked towards Jackie who nodded at her.

- Yes, much more than you know.

- I'm very glad to hear that. Your return is a positivity.

Sketch smiled. As much as she didn't want to leave it hadn't occurred to her that they would have noticed her absence within the computer.

She turned and hugged Jackie for the final time.

"Bye."

As she held her friend in her arms she began to fade leaving only a warm feeling between Jackie's outstretched arms.

"Goodbye Sketch, I'll miss you," whispered Jackie wiping away a tear that escaped from the side of her eye.

After worlds

Chapter 29

"FEELS LIKE SOMETHING'S MISSING, doesn't it?" said Trevor. Monday morning was minus both sausage sarnies and Sketch.

"And it's raining," said Begw scrunching up her face as she took a sip of her coffee. "You've put more than half a teaspoon of milk in this."

Trevor shrugged. "Will they be alright without her? Will we be alright without her?"

"Yes, of course, we will. Man up, Trevor," said Begw watching her coffee spiral away down the plug hole of the staffroom sink. "What time are the people I don't know about who are campaigning against the closure they don't know about arriving?"

"Ten thirty I believe," Trevor said glancing at the clock on the staff room wall. The little hand was approaching ten; the big hand sat at ten fifteen. "Which means they'll be arriving any minute now."

"Best look all positive then."

Begw felt anything but, the odds of winning the fight against the closure remained slim. There had been successful cases in other parts of the country which had kept library services open but left their budgets slashed, they were run by volunteer and had limited opening hours. With Sketch gone, Begw began to wonder whether there would even be a campaign.

Leaving the staff room, Begw saw a long queue of people formed outside of the entrance to the library.

"It's unbelievable how many people are out there just to save a few books," said Trevor. "This is the busiest we've been in years."

"I think it's got less to do with books and more to do with a sense of community and of course Sketch."

Begw opened up and let everyone in from the cold and then absented herself, still keeping the facade that she had no idea what was going on.

Under the leadership of Mr Moore, the group's numbers had spiralled in the last few days making the library busier than ever. Over the course of the weekend, the message about the planned closure leaked out via electronic Chinese whispers. Hashtag #save-NCSLibrary began popping up on local Twitter feeds and had been picked up by activists dedicated to campaigning against the ongoing storm which threatened to wipe out libraries across the country.

"Welcome, welcome all," said Mr Moore.

A ripple of hush shimmered across the room as the crowd of locals directed their attention to him.

"Thanks for coming out on this miserable December day. I know lots of people couldn't be here this morning because of work or school, but they've been emailing me with updates and pledges of support."

As one of the stars of the Silver Surfers course, Mr Moore regularly checked his email on the tablet his wife bought him as an early Christmas present.

"The protest will take place on Friday evening, so more people can join in; them at school and work. Today, we'll work in teams to drum up more interest. Be sure to let people know to be here by six before the library officially closes for the day." He checked down a list on his tablet. "Can we have two or three volunteers to be in charge of refreshments? It might be a long night."

Three hands shot up offering tea, biscuits, Portuguese custard tarts and Battenberg cake.

"Thank you," he nodded. "I'll leave leaflets out on the side and if everyone can organise into groups of two or three - safety in numbers. I think that's about it. Any questions?"

"What about all the tweets and stuff?" asked Rochelle. "Won't the council read them?"

"Since when did they listen to anything the good old public have to say?" laughed Mr Moore. "Anyway, the more noise we make, the harder it will be for them to ignore us."

❅

"MUM," shouted Matt from the living room.

"Mum?"

"Hold on Matt," said Jackie who was upstairs decorating the office to make it into a room for Ashling and Sammy who were due to move in before Christmas.

She ambled downstairs, not noticing as she wiped emulsion paint across the side of her face.

"What is it, Matt? I could do with a cuppa if you are making one."

"It's the computer, it's dead," said Matt.

Jackie froze. What about Sketch? If the PC had stopped working what did that mean for her? It had been hard enough getting used to the idea she was gone but the knowledge Sketch was alive inside the computer, albeit in a different form, made it bearable. If the computer was damaged, did that mean she was hurt or even gone?

"Mum!"

"Sorry Matt, err have you tried restarting it?"

"I'm not stupid. Of course, I have."

Jackie believed him, but this didn't prevent her from attempting to reboot the machine.

"Make me some tea, Matt."

He sighed and switched on the kettle.

Rebooting had no effect, there was still no power, no light and no sign of any energy.

"Does this mean we can get a new one?" asked Matt.

"No, we're going to get this fixed," snapped Jackie. "Get me my address book, and I'll ring that man who looked at it last time."

Chapter 30

BRITNEY STARED at her phone's Facebook app aghast. She threw her mobile at the wall, making a dull bang. *A baby, he'd had a baby with that skank.* Everyone knew her guy had a kid except for her because her so-called boyfriend failed to tell her. Did she matter so little to him?

Never liked him that much anyway, she said to herself. *He'll get what's coming to him, and it's not going to be me.*

She recovered her phone from the far side of the room, its screen cracked, splintering the image of her locked in a tongue-twisting snog with Matt.

"Daddy, I'm going to need a new phone," said Britney adopting her best distressed daughter tone. She pulled out her tablet from under a pile of discarded clothing and messaged Rochelle, inviting herself over to her friend's house.

Rochelle was spending a lot more time with Britney. In the last couple of weeks, Britney started messaging all the time, wanting to hang out and walk to school with her. The sudden attention surprised her, but she'd put a lot of time into to making herself more popular and being friends with Britney didn't hurt.

The pair were sprawled across Britney's bed watching YouTube clips and laughing at people on Facebook.

"Roch?" said Britney putting the tablet down and facing her friend. "You know your brother?"

"I should do, been stuck with him for seventeen years. He's so annoying. If he didn't look the spit of dad, I'd swear they'd adopted him."

"Thing is...well, is he seeing anyone?" asked Britney twizzling her hair around her finger.

"Hashtag LOL," said Rochelle. "That's a good one Britney. Why would anyone go out with my brother? He's a minger."

"I'm serious. Dominic might be your brother, but he's fit."

Rochelle covered her mouth and nostrils to prevent her from snorting in a loud, ugly fashion.

"Whatevs. He's been hanging out with that what's her face; you know the one who had a kid. Errr Ashley."

"Ashling," corrected Britney. She fluffed up her hair and stuck out her chest. "She's got no chance against me."

"What about Matt?"

"What about him? I only went with him for a laugh, but he was dull as so I binned him."

Rochelle shook her head, "And now you're interested in Dominic? You're such a joker."

"Invite me round for dinner tomorrow," said Britney, "And watch him turn to boy putty in my hands."

"Eurrrgh!"

❄

MATT THREW an empty crisp packet at the bin, growling as it missed its target. There was no way anyone was going to fix their computer. Even if they did it would only break down again next week. He'd thought about asking his dad to get him one, but after the revelation that he was Sammy's father, his dad was furious at him. There'd had a huge row, with lots of shouting about how irresponsible he'd been, that he'd ruined his future. His dad wasn't

Life in your world

about to do him any favours. But Matt needed a computer for school, especially with the possibility of the library closing. His mum arranged for an "IT specialist" to come around that evening. If Matt's experience of Jackie's specialists was anything to go by, he'd be a man who taught himself some basics in the back room and decided to put an ad in the window of the Kentish Town grocery store.

The day sucked. He'd been round to Dominic's, but when he walked in the front door, he came face-to-face with Britney. She'd shot him a foul look as she brushed past him on her way upstairs, not even saying "hi". After that, he didn't fancy hanging around for long. His list of things to do didn't include facing up to an angry Britney. What had he seen in the girl? Everything about her seemed superficial now. Dominic convinced him to stay, handing him a games console controller. Despite the distraction of a virtual world where he could shoot things with no consequence thoughts whirled around in Matt's mind. His house was weird. Everything in his life was changing. He'd had little time to get used to Sketch's return to wherever she lived, and now Ashling and Sammy were poised to move in. This stuff messed with his head. Why couldn't everything stay how it was.

Between rounds of fighting a fictional enemy, he attempted to share his thoughts with Dominic.

"Thing is, I've not spoken to her much for so long that I don't know what to say. Before you say anything, I know that's my fault, but even though Sammy is mine, I don't know how to be a dad. I've got no clue."

"Yeh, I can't imagine it myself, but he's a cute kid, easy to get on with, not like some of them. Just play with him."

"Suppose, but what do I say to him?"

Dominic sighed. "I dunno. You've just got to get to know him. Take him to the park or something."

Matt couldn't help but think it wasn't going to be quite as straightforward as that. What did he know about kids?

Chapter 31

BRITNEY LEFT ROCHELLE'S HOUSE, filled with ice cream, chicken tikka masala and lashings of glee. She relished the way Matt looked when they met in the hallway like he wished they were still together. *Like that was ever going to happen,* she thought. Having an invitation to dinner presented her the ideal opportunity to gather the information necessary to put her revenge plan into action. It meant spending time with boring Rochelle and her family, but everything good had a price, didn't it?

The conversation crisscrossed the Ikea dinner table, providing revealing gems of information.

"This is delicious, Mrs Martin."

"Thanks, Britney, but do call me Pam," said Rochelle's mum. "It's one of our Dominic's favourites."

"Where is he anyway?" asked Rochelle, keen to make sure Britney got to have some time with her brother even though the thought of anyone kissing her brother still made her icky.

"Finishing up some of the stuff for the save the library business," said Pam.

"The what business?" asked Britney.

"The council want to shut it down," said Rochelle. "We're trying to stop it. Me, Dominic, Matt and some others, with a bunch of old people."

"Going to have a sit-in starting Friday night," said Pam inbetween mouthfuls of rice and curry. "Reminds me of the eighties, all those demos about miners and the poll tax."

"Imagine that," said Britney. "Can anyone join in?"

Britney excused herself and went upstairs on the premise of going to the toilet. Instead of using the loo, she hovered outside Dominic's bedroom listening to the muffled voices on the other side. Despite the door, she overheard Matt confide his doubts about fatherhood to Dominic.

Britney didn't go to school the next day. Her dad emailed the school after she looked distraught, clutched her stomach and mentioned women's problems. She had more pressing things to do than dissecting the contents of Great Expectations, things involving the flyer Rochelle's mum handed to her before Britney left the night before and a bunch of emails from a fake email address. Scanning the A5 glossy paper, she smiled to herself at the thought of ruining Matt. Brittany composed an email using an account she'd set up in his name to some old bloke called Winston who, according to the council's website was the Head of the Library Service.

After penning her email missive to the council, Britney put the next part of her plan into action, hacking into Matt's online accounts; she never went out with anyone without finding out their passwords. She grabbed her coat and headed out into the bustle of London's streets. By eleven thirty, she stood outside Ashling's building repeatedly pressing the buzzer for her flat.

"Hello?"

"Hi Ashling, it's Britney."

"Er, hi," said Ashling.

"Can I come up?"

Sounds of static came through the buzzer. Britney's plan counted on her talking to Ashling. She glared at the intercom willing it to buzz.

"Ashling? You still there? It's important." She heard a sigh.

"It's the third floor. Come up."

Britney scanned the hallway of Ashling's flat, trying to wheedle her way out of the corridor and into the living room, but Ashling stood her ground. Britney harboured little sympathy for the young mum and took pleasure in announcing Matt was spreading rumours about Ashling.

"I don't believe you," said Ashling.

"Sorry, I really am, but it's true. Matt told me last night after, well you know after what."

Ashling found herself shrinking into the sofa, feeling somewhat smaller than she had fifteen minutes before when she still believed things were going to change, when there was hope of a better life than just changing nappies and struggling to make ends meet on meagre benefits.

"But I'm moving in there. He said he believed me now."

Britney moved to put her arm around Ashling.

"Don't," said Ashling, shrugging her off.

"Thing is he doesn't believe that gorgeous little Sam there is his."

"It's Sammy."

"Ok, Sammy. Even if he is the father, do you think it's going to work you living in the same house as him when he thinks you've lied about it all?" asked Britney. She was tempted just to give Ashling a good slap.

Ashling shrugged.

"What's it got to do with you anyway?"

"Think about it. Matt's going to resent you living there. It's going to make things impossible for you. Not just you, but Sammy as well," said Britney.

"Look, Britney, I appreciate you coming around to tell me all this, but I think you should go now. I'm sure Matt is waiting for you."

After Britney had left, Ashling looked around her dingy half-packed flat wondering what the hell to do. She didn't want to be with Matt, but this wasn't the right place to bring up a kid. Hadn't he split up with Britney anyway? Had she been stupid to trust them and believe everything was going to have a happy ending? Life didn't have happy endings. She opened a bag full of Sammy's clothes and began to unpack them.

❄

FRIDAY MORNING PROVED to be as cold and wintry as previous December days, but the Christmas decorations in shop windows and hoisted across the streets of Kentish Town brought a hue of brightness. The determined library campaigners set information points outside local train and rail stations, handing out homemade flyers spreading the word about the protest at the library later that day. Discarded sheets of paper, abandoned by commuters littered the gutters of surrounding pavements, but now and again someone stopped to talk to the campaigners, pledging their support and promising to turn up at the protest.

The group reconvened in a local café as the rush hour crowds subsided, rewarding themselves with warming coffee and cake.

"Some of these people are so rude. Shoving passed at high speed. You'd think they wanted to go to work," said Flo, tucking into a slice of lemon drizzle cake.

"They're not all like that. I had a chat with a lovely man who said he'd practically grown up in the library. Said he would finish up a book in a day and head back to get a new one. Used to use the encyclopaedias to do his homework as well," said Mrs Harding-Edgar.

Mr Barrington giggled.

"What?" said Flo.

His giggles turned to raucous laughter, distracting people from their lattes and flat whites.

General mirth took hold, infecting the campaigners one-by-one until they were all at the mercy of uncontrollable laughter.

"What are we? What are? What are we laughing about?" asked Flo trying to regain some semblance of sobriety.

"I don't know," choked Mr Barrington.

❄

Life in your world

WINSTON OBILOGUI WAS TIRED. He was five years off retirement having worked for the local authority for twenty years, or as he liked to think of it about nineteen years too long. Over the course of two decades, he'd seen it all, boom, bust, cuts, crazy schemes to change the lives of local residents who either didn't know about them or had violently opposed to them. He'd considered leaving many times, more frequently of late now there was no large, shiny pension to look forward to, but what else could he do? Better to hang on in there, buried in bureaucracy than having to re-establish himself elsewhere.

The announcement from above of the latest round of cuts messed up his plans to begin winding down. Now he faced closing half the library provision in the borough. So far, they'd managed to keep it under the radar and away from campaigners, but he knew it was a matter of when rather than if it some disgruntled council employee who thought they could change the world with a bit of banner waving and petitions leaked it. The Occupy London movement, which had entrenched itself in the heart of the capital, had a lot to answer for.

At eleven o'clock, Winston considered his priorities for the rest of the day, knowing he had a stack of unread emails he should address. The thought made him shudder. It wasn't early enough to eat his fruit-based packed lunch, but he could justify a cup of coffee. He relished the chance to head out to the nearest coffee conglomerate for an extra-large butterscotch latte topped with a big dollop of cream. Emails could wait until later. He grabbed his coat and scarf and headed out the door but was stopped by his assistant.

"Have you seen that email Winston?" she said looking worried.

"Later Marilyn. I'm just off for an important meeting. I should be back before lunch, but if not I'll look at it this afternoon."

"But..."

Before she could finish her sentence, he strode off across the room leaving her wondering if she should go after him but Winston was famous for his sudden rages, so she decided against it.

Chapter 32

JACKIE TOOK the afternoon off work to finish off the transformation of the spare room into a lovely space for Ashling and Sammy, before going to join the library sit-in later in the afternoon. The house still seemed empty, and she felt like by making the changes she was erasing all remaining traces of Sketch.

Last night's visit by the IT man confirmed her worst fears. After fifteen minutes looking at the PC, he agreed reluctantly to take it away to attempt a repair. He hadn't held out much hope of success. Jackie felt she'd sent Sketch to her end by letting her return to the Core. What made it worse was Sketch had had such reservations about her going back. *Maybe she'd sensed something was wrong*, thought Jackie. The "what ifs" were beginning to take over Jackie's thought patterns. What if she'd asked her to stay? What if she'd insisted they do more tests to make sure the transformation would work? What if she'd never got involved in this in the first place? If she'd got the computer fixed ages ago, Sketch would be safe instead of dead?

"Mum, it's time to go," shouted Matt from the ground floor.

She pulled herself back from her spiralling anxiety. The least she could do was to help to save the library. That would be a fitting memorial to Sketch.

"Okay, be right there."

The pair headed down the road towards the library.

"Mum, do you have an email address for Sketch? Her Facebook account has been deactivated. I thought at first she'd just unfriended me, but she's nowhere to be found online."

"Really?" said Jackie. "I'm must have somewhere."

"Or a mobile number for her mum? That's how she ended up staying with us, wasn't it? Because her mum's an old friend of yours."

"I'll have a look when we get in."

Matt wasn't convinced. His mum was acting a bit shifty. Like the time when she didn't want to tell him his dad had moved out. She'd pretended he was at a conference for three days and had only fessed up when he failed to return at the weekend.

"So, what's really going on then," he said stopping in the middle of the street.

"What do you mean?"

"Come on mum; it works both ways. If I'm not allowed to lie to you, then you should tell me the truth too."

Jackie looked at her watch. They still had time before they needed to be at the library and maybe this was more important.

"Ok," she said, sighing. "Let's go and sit in the cafe across the road, and I'll tell you."

❄

WINSTON OBILOGUI nearly didn't go back to the office. It was Friday afternoon, and there was nothing urgent on his to-do list that wouldn't languish there until Monday. However, his Blackberry and Marilyn appeared not to have signed up to this brilliant plan. A string of texts and email alerts, which he worked very hard to ignore punctuated his lunch break. He dismissed them as trivial, probably a photocopier malfunctioned somewhere or a book consignment stuck in traffic. However, given he was Head of the Library Service he decided he should get back and show his face for an hour or so. He could always fill the rest of the afternoon playing games on his computer.

He sneaked in as Marilyn was in the full flow of conversation with a colleague, wanting to avoid any more harassment from her. On his keyboard sat a piece of paper with a message written in black marker pen. It read, "There's going to be a protest at Kentish Town library". Taped underneath it was a copy of the flyer the campaigners had been distributing earlier in the day.

"Marilyn," he shouted. "Get in here now."

His assistant walked in pan-faced.

"Can I help you with something, Winston?"

"Why didn't you tell me about this?"

Marilyn sighed.

"Get me Begw Jones on the phone now."

❄

MATT WONDERED what you did when one of your parents started to display signs of mental illness. Who did you call? He wasn't about to ring up the police and say his mum thought people lived inside the computer.

"But there's nothing in the computer, Mum. I mean, not nothing, but there's just microchips, processors and electrical wires. But there are no mysterious people, hidden between the bits of metal, making things work," he said.

"That's just it Matt; they aren't people. They're energies, energies that cluster together to make things happen. Sketch is…was one of those. She was an energy."

"Sketch is a person, a real-life, living person. I even believed I fancied her at one point."

"You fancy everyone," said Jackie attempting a halfhearted smile.

"Mum, Sketch is real. Even if she was one of these…energies how could she have come out of the computer?"

"They can transform from one energy form to another. Kind of like teleporting but they change form as they go," said Jackie.

"That's just bonkers mum. Anyway, the computer's broken."

"Exactly, why do you think I'm so worried? Why do you think I'm telling you this?"

"I don't know," said Matt, wondering if life would ever settle down. He suspected not.

"I need you to try and fix the computer. It's the only way we might be able to save her," said Jackie.

Chapter 33

BEGW SAT SLUMPED on a chair in the staffroom making small snorting noises under her breath. She didn't want to let on to the group of people beginning to congregate in the cafe area, but it seemed like the game was up.

"What did he say?" asked Trevor.

"He said he was coming over and he sounded very pissed off."

"Did he say why?"

"Do they ever? No, they just say 'I'm coming over' and then let you stew in it. I can make a fair guess though, can't you?" said Begw flicking her fringe out of her eyes. It was way overdue a trim, but with everything going on she'd not managed to find the time.

"Best get out there Trevor. Wouldn't be done to be seen slacking with Mister Big Boss coming over."

The pair jumped as a loud knock came at the door.

"Jones," said Winston, nodding at Trevor.

Trevor winked at Begw, hoping that it conveyed "good luck, you'll be ok and Winston is an idiot" before leaving the room.

"You were very clearly told to keep this under wraps, Jones," said Winston. "Then I find you've been organising a protest, a sit-in to boot."

"I've not organised anything, boss. Not a memo has been sent. In fact, I'm not aware of any sit-in to boot," she said, looking him straight in the eye.

"Not aware my foot," said Trevor.

"Was that pun intended?" she asked with a quick wink to her colleague.

"Let me be clear; there will be no sit-in, no protest or anything of its ilk here today or any other day. Security are on their way."

"Now don't you think you're going too far? You'll have the TV crews down here in a flash if anything happens to those old dears," she said beginning to feel the rage of injustice flowing through her welsh blood.

"I don't much care what you think young lady. You are suspended pending a formal enquiry into the leak of the closure," he said.

"Proposed closure."

"Oh, it's going to happen alright. Not because I want it to but because it has to. Now give me the keys please and go home."

Begw regained her composure, resisting an urge to slam the door on her way out. She swerved passed Trevor who had the look of a man who'd been listening to their conversation with his ear against the door.

"I need you to keep an eye on things here for me," she whispered, hurrying past.

Winston got out his laptop and began to document the details of his meeting with Begw and its outcome. He couldn't help think the world had been a better place without all this modern technology. All it had done was to increase the expectation you could do paperwork any time, any place. He didn't get to finish documenting the events before he was interrupted by Trevor.

"Your security people are here," he scowled.

"Good, good," said Winston leaving the room. "Get the kettle on then. I'm parched."

Trevor humphed. While he didn't mind making drinks on demand for Begw, he drew the line at doing anything to help the man who was conspiring to get rid of them both.

He sat down on the chair in front of Winston's computer.

"Now then, what do we have here? Oh, my fingers have stumbled upon Mr Winston's emails, and now I'm going to read them accidentally."

❄

MATT DIDN'T KNOW what to believe as his mum told him the story of how she'd got involved with the energies in the first place. They'd forgotten they were supposed to be at the library for the protest until Matt caught a glimpse of the red of Ashling's coat through the cafe window.

"Come on, there's Ashling and Sammy," he said putting his coat on. "We're late. If you want to, we can carry on talking about these energy things later."

Jackie paid for their coffees as Matt dashed up out to catch Ashling before she got too far ahead.

"Hey Sammy," he said looking down to the pushchair with a small sense of pride. He'd helped to make him.

"Don't talk to him," said Ashling.

"What? What's wrong with you this time?" asked Matt.

"You pretending you want to be his dad, making out you're happy for us to come and live with you and then telling everyone else something completely different."

"I have no idea what you are talking about," protested Matt.

" There I was, convinced she was making it up, then I saw your post," said Ashling close to tears. She pulled her phone from her pocket and held it up to his face.

"What's this?" asked Jackie, emerging from the cafe.

Ashling's Facebook timeline displayed a post from Matt declaring she was a ho who was trying to worm her way into his family by pretending he was the father of her child.

Matt froze and went the palest shade possible for his skin tone.

"I didn't write that," he said.

"It's pretty evident you did," said Ashling. "Just stay away from us."

"Matt," began Jackie.

"Honestly mum, I didn't."

Ashling raced to the traffic lights and managing to cross before Matt and Jackie could catch up with her. Between the cars, buses and dangerous cyclists, they were stuck there until the lights changed from amber to green again.

"What am I going to do?" asked Matt.

"Don't worry, if you are telling the truth we'll get to the bottom of it," said Jackie putting her arm around her son. Something told her he wasn't lying about this.

"I'm am."

❄

AT FOUR THIRTY pm on a Friday in December, it was dark on the streets of Kentish Town, or it would have been had there not been rows and rows of shops and other retail outlets helping the street lamps to illuminate the area. Despite the dark and cold, the road bustled with people leaving work, heading home or going out with friends and colleagues. At that time of day, it was always busy with speed walkers, but pedestrian congestion seemed worse than usual. A crowd gathered outside the library. The only people who remained inside were Trevor, members of the security team and Winston, who had decided the best way of preventing the sit-in was to close early.

"Let us in, young man," said Flo. "It's not like we are going to do any damage."

The security guard shrugged.

"Sorry love, the library's shut for today. Come back tomorrow for your books."

"What do you mean it's shut? It's only half past," shouted Rochelle Martin from the back of the group. She pushed her way towards the front followed by Mr Moore who was keen to have his say too.

"Just closed," said the Security Guard.

"The lights are still on. I want to speak to Miss Jones," demanded Mr Moore.

"I've just been told the library's closed. If you want to speak to anyone come back tomorrow."

"That's not good enough," said Jackie who had just arrived. She was in no mood for any more nonsense. "We want to speak to Begw. Who do we want to speak to?" she asked the small crowd of supporters?

"Begw," came the collective reply.

"When do we want to speak to her?"

"Now."

The crowd turned from a hopeful bunch of book borrowers to an agitated group of protesters determined to have their way. As the chanting got louder, people began to crowd around them, standing on tip-toes to get a better view of what was going on. There was nothing like a bit of free street entertainment on a Friday afternoon. Before long smartphones captured much of the action, by way of photos and videos, sharing them across the Internet.

Inside the building, Winston raged. Surely they all knew they were wasting their time. Not just their time but their taxpayer's money too. It was going to put an increasing dent in his already overstretched budget to keep security there much longer. He didn't want to have to pay them overtime.

"What are they shouting about?" he said, barking at Trevor who was busy retweeting things on Twitter to make sure as many people knew about the protest as possible.

"They want Begw. They trust her."

"Well, they're not going to get what they want. She's not here, is she?" said Winston. "You'll have to go out and talk to them instead."

"Me?" said Trevor.

"Yes, you. Get out there and tell the protesters," Winston sneered. "Ms Jones no longer works here, tell them all to go home."

The security guards were having a tough time keeping control of the crowd of angry people. The older they were, the more aggressive they appeared to be. All it took to incur an injury was a subtle slip of a walking stick at the wrong angle, and it would be near on impossible to pinpoint who was responsible.

The door to the library edged open revealing an uncertain Trevor.

"Hello, everyone. I'm afraid Begw isn't here just now, and we've had to shut early," he paused. "Sod it. They've given her the sack or near about. Trying to keep us all quiet."

"Well we're not going anywhere," said Mr Barrington. "Everyone, if they won't let us inside, let's all just sit down here on the pavement."

He levered himself down to the ground damp with the chill of winter in the air. Jackie and Trevor followed suit, and soon most of the crowd did the same.

Watching from behind a bookcase, Winston groaned out loud and pressed the nuclear button on his phone, calling in the local police. Doing so meant the protest would make the news and he'd be lucky to make it to retirement.

The Met police force was not unaccustomed to dealing with unruly behaviour on the streets, be it Friday night or Tuesday morning, but they were rarely called out to remove a bunch of pensioners and teenagers linked together on the streets calling for their library to be reopened. Whilst less obnoxious than office workers binge drinking to blot out the boredom of their week, the community protest was still an inauspicious start to the evening.

"Unhand me, young woman," demanded an old lady with a pointy umbrella. "I'll have you know my mother was a suffragette. Activism is in my blood."

"That maybe," said the PC, "But you can't sit here all night blocking up the pathway. Besides anything else, you'll freeze to death. It's going to be a cold one according to the forecast."

The old lady grinned back at him defiantly. "We've got our love to keep us warm," she said gripping even tighter to the two, young people on either side of her.

There appeared to be a standoff. The police had no objection to forcibly removing teenagers and adults, but they were reluctant to do the same with frail, older people. It would do damage to their public image, not to mention that the older protesters reminded them of their own ageing relatives.

"Come on love; you've had your say. Why not organise a petition or something like that? You need to have a permit to have a demo."

"Bah, this isn't a demo. It's a sit-in, and we're going to sit-in for as long as it takes for that man in there to give us back our library."

"Pop and get us a coffee," said the PC to his subordinate. "Looks like we are going to be here for a while."

Chapter 34

BEGW WAS in the Pineapple getting drunk as fast as she could with a line of tequila shots in front of her when she noticed her phone ringing.

"Shut up with the ringing. There's nothing I can do," she said to it through the cloth of her bag. "I tried and look where it's got me."

The call terminated, but seconds later the phone started to ring again.

Begw sighed. "Alright, I asked you nicely if that's the way you want it I'll switch you off."

She dipped her hand into her bag, pulling out the offending object.

"Oh."

The face on her phone was not one she'd been expecting to see.

"Hello." She listened through the cloud of spirits that had taken control of her brain. "Oh."

"Give me a glass of water," she said to the barman. "I've got things to do."

The midst of an angry protest wasn't the best place for Matt to attempt to talk with Ashling but he didn't know what was going on.

She had positioned herself close to the window by Dominic. The pair glared at Matt as he approached them.

"Surprised to see you showing your face here," said Dominic. "I know what you did."

"I haven't done anything," said Matt, still not able to get his head around what might be going on. "I've no idea what everyone thinks I've done now."

"Oh I think you do," said Ashling pulling Sammy closer to her.

"I don't. Why don't you just tell me?" he asked looking from one to another before turning to Dominic "I really don't know what you think I've done to Ashling but swear I didn't mean to hurt anyone."

"You didn't mean to hurt anyone? By emailing the Head of the Library Service to tell them Begw had orchestrated a demonstration?" said Dominic.

Matt's mouth gaped open. Where was all this coming from? He hadn't even seen his email today. He'd been in lessons all morning, at home in the afternoon with the broken computer and then listening to his mum's crazy theories about Sketch.

"I have no clue what you're talking about," he said.

"You think you can bluff your way out of this one, but you can't. Trevor saw the email you sent on Winston's laptop," said Dominic. "Why don't you just take off and leave us all alone? You've done enough damage."

The tequila Begw consumed gave her the illusion of warmth, but she couldn't help but be concerned about the group of old people stationed outside the library. It was time to put a stop to this. She wasn't going to have death by hypothermia on her hands no matter how many book borrowing facilities were at risk.

"Oi," she shouted above the chanting. Slowly the noise around her subsided until the sound of the traffic had regained its prominence.

Mr Barrington beamed, "Miss Jones."

"Call me Begw, Mr B. Right everyone. I know things seem bleak but what I need you do to is to stand up and take yourselves off home for tonight."

The people began to protest.

"No, no, I appreciate what you've all done, but you can't do any more tonight. Trust me. I'm on it," she said.

"Begw," said Dominic. "I know who did this."

"Save it. We've got bigger fish to fry."

The crowd began to disperse, in part relieved that they could get warmed up but cold inside with the feeling they had somehow failed to make any difference. It was a grim end to the week.

Chapter 35

OVER THE WEEKEND, the repercussions of previous week continued. Those who had been at the library on Friday evening remained frustrated by their lack of power to change anything. Some were angry, others unhappy, and the failure of the sit-in coloured all their moods in the days to come.

Matt tried to talk to Ashling, but she refused to answer her phone or the buzzer for her flat.

"You just need to give her time," said Jackie serving up her best helping of support accompanied by cups of tea.

"What good's that going to do? None of this is anything to do with me."

"I know hon. I know."

Like it or not, his mum was the only one who seemed to believe he hadn't slept with Britney or that he hadn't denied being Sammy's dad. Nor did he know who had been sending emails to the council in his name.

Britney called him on Saturday morning when he was still in bed. She left a voicemail, angling to meet up with him. He suspected she wanted them to get back together, but he wasn't keen.

She'd been less than supportive when she'd found out about Sammy, catty and mean even. He could do without her calls. It was Ashling he wanted to hear from.

His phone beeped at him making his heart race. Could it be her? Would she talk to him? The message came from a withheld number. Matt opened up the message from the unknown source. It read,

- *Please meet on Monday at seven pm at Community Centre, in Busby Place. All your questions will be answered.*

The text gave no name. Instead, it was signed off with the words "A friend".

"Mum, look at this?" he said handing her his ageing mobile. "Who do you think it's from?"

"That's odd," she said. "I just got one too. It's the same as yours. No idea who sent it."

"Should we go? I mean, it's weird, isn't it?"

"I agree, but we should go. It'll be okay. There's two of us," said Jackie.

The mysterious nature of the texts received by Jackie and Matt gave them something else to think about but were not enough to wipe away their worries about Ashling and Sammy. Speculation as to who sent them made them curious enough to arrive at the Community Centre ahead of time. Despite being early, they discovered lights on in the building and chatter coming from the interior.

Jackie knocked. They waited, eyeing each other and the door until they heard the distinctive sounds of keys unlocking, allowing them entry to the hall.

"Begw," said Matt inching passed the librarian into the relative warmth of the building with his mum. "Was it you who sent us the texts then?"

"Nope, not me. All will be revealed shortly," said the short Welsh woman, dressed in a dark trouser suit and sporting a freshly trimmed fringe.

Life in your world

A further knock at the door heralded an influx of people, many of whom Jackie recognised from the previous Friday's aborted sit-in.

"Must be about the library, all this," she said to Matt who nodded. He located chairs for them towards the back of the room.

"No, let's sit nearer to the front."

"Do we have to?" he asked.

"Yes."

Ashling was also in attendance with Sammy. She scanned around the room working out how best to sit as far away from Matt and Jackie as possible. Her line of vision trained itself onto Britney, but before they made eye contact, she saw Trevor waving at her.

"What's she doing here?" asked Trevor as Ashling sat down next to him and Dominic.

"No idea. Not like she cares about books or anything much apart from herself," said Ashling. "Mind you, she did tell me about Matt."

"Warned you off more like," said Trevor.

"She can't be all bad then."

Begw stood up and cleared her throat. The sound emerging wasn't very loud, so she went back to her default "Oi". It had a consistent success rate in gaining the attention of a crowd.

"Thanks all for coming and for what you all tried to do on Friday. The reason I've got you all gathered here is because I received a very important phone call last week. One that might just help us to keep the library open." She paused, scanning the room to check everyone was listening. "The call was from someone who gave me the number of a lawyer who wants to help us. In fact, he spoke to one of you on Friday morning at the Tube station."

"Oh, oh, that was me," said Mr Barrington standing up and shaking his hands with excitement. "I think."

"It was indeed. Let me introduce you all to Mr Neil James," said Begw.

A wave of applause and a random whoop rippled across the room as a man in his mid-thirties wearing a designer suit and showing the early signs of balding, stood up from one of the chairs on the front row.

"Good evening everyone. I'm here tonight because I think there are sufficient grounds to stop the go ahead of the library closure, at least in the short-term." He held up a sheet of paper. "This outlines the recent case of Lincolnshire County Council who were ruled against last week in a high court judgment regarding the closure of their library service."

There were murmurs throughout the room.

"How many of you were consulted on the changes the council is proposing to make?"

No hands were raised, and everyone in the hall remained silent.

"No one? Well, in which case we have an excellent case to stop this in its tracks. The judge ruled that another County Council failed to consult properly with stakeholders and therefore their plans were illegal."

A second wave of clapping erupted across the room.

"There's a lot of work to do, and the very first thing I will advocate for is that Ms Jones gets her suspension lifted," said Neil.

"And we need some volunteers to make up an action committee," added Begw standing up again.

Hands sprang up.

"Can everyone put their names and contact details on the form I'm about to circulate? We'll find a role for you all in the campaign. Don't worry about that," she said.

"Begw," said Jackie from the front row. "There's something I want to set straight with everyone." She turned to face the rest of the gathering.

"My Matt didn't send that email to the council. He's not perfect, but it's just not something he'd do."

"But Trevor saw it," said Dominic rising from his chair. "Why do you both keep lying about it?"

"He's not lying," said a voice from the corner of the room. Jackie jumped up, eyes darting around until she found its source.

"Sketch!"

Sketch strolled across the hall, not stopping to say hello or acknowledge her friends. When she reached the front of those assembled, she stood and surveyed the room.

Life in your world

"Things are not always what they seem," she said. "It's true that the Head of the Library service received an email from Matt disclosing the details of the protest, but he didn't send it."

All eyes were upon Sketch.

"Some of you may know who I am and you are probably surprised to see me as I was supposed to leave London last week," she looked towards Jackie and Matt.

"I very nearly did. I came very close to going home but then I realised there were things I had to finish. Someone once told me endings are important. That lady was called Maud. Maud didn't get to say goodbye, to sort things out before she left but I do so that's why I am here."

"Never mind all that. Who sent the email?" shouted a ginger haired man from the middle row of seats.

Britney cowered in her chair, pulling her scarf around her face as an added layer of protection. Surely there was no way the stupid, skinny girl who'd been living at Matt's house could know it what she'd done.

"The person who sent it is," Sketch paused, unable to bring herself to share the information in such a public space.

"Tell us then," came a voice from the crowd.

"I..." said Sketch. She looked around for a trusted face, a person to help her avoid this awkwardness.

"I'm going to share what I know with someone. They can verify it for you. The important thing is you know it wasn't Matt, not who it was."

She turned to Begw Jones and beckoned her over. From out of her bag she pulled a crumpled piece of paper containing the details of an IP address search and showed it to Begw. The Librarian scrutinised it line by line.

"Okay, it's not the boy Matt," she said. "He's in the clear."

The tension in the room began to disperse, and with the hotness removed from the air, the focus returned to the matter of the library. Neil the lawyer, outlined the next steps including reiterating his intention to have Begw reinstated to the role of Library Manager.

With business concluded, the attendees began to leave in dribs and drabs, all of them happier and more hopeful than when they had arrived, except for Britney who attempted to make a swift and unseen departure from the hall. Sketch noticed her trying to sneak away behind a small group of teenagers.

"Can I talk to you?"

With Jackie, Matt, Ashling and Dominic clustered around Sketch, the last thing Britney wanted to do was to go anywhere near her. Sketch could expose her at any time, so she continued to head for the door pretending not to have heard her.

Sketch turned back to her group of friends.

"You're okay." said Jackie with relief evident in her voice.

"Yes, sorry if I worried you but I'll tell you all about it later. First I need to set a few things straight," said Sketch.

"What did you want with Britney?" asked Matt. Ashling glared at him at the mention of her nemesis.

"To give her the benefit of the doubt. I was hoping she'd tell you herself."

"Tell us what?" said Ashling.

"That it was her who sent the email. I'm guessing she was jealous of you and Matt becoming closer," said Sketch.

"But why?" asked Ashling. "They're back together."

"And Ashling is *my* girlfriend," said Dominic causing Ashling to blush.

"Err, I don't know what you think you know Ashling, but I broke up with Britney ages ago," said Matt.

Everyone looked from Matt to Ashling then to Sketch as a flurry of pennies began to drop like hailstones.

"You didn't sleep with her?"

Matt shook his head.

"Or tell her you didn't want to have anything to do with Sammy?"

"No," said Matt. "Look, I want to get to know Sammy, that's the most important thing to me. We still want you to come and live with us, don't we mum?"

"Of course we do. Room's sorted and everything," said Jackie.

Begw joined the group and suggested they all continued the

conversation in the pub around the corner. The hall hire period was coming to an end, and she fancied a pint. Reconvening at the Pineapple over alcoholic drinks, they raked over the bones of the meeting and put aside their misconceptions.

"Can we move in tomorrow," asked Ashling after all the questions about the library and Britney's deceit had been answered.

"Cool, but what about you Sketch? Where are you going to stay?"

Sketch pointed at Trevor whose grin stretched across his face.

"Just where I've been since I left, in Trevor's spare room. That's how I've managed to stay in touch with all the developments about the library."

"I've got a freezer full of frozen sausages now," he said with an exaggerated wink.

Jackie took Sketch to one side.

"Can I have a word?"

"Of course," said Sketch. "You must have a million questions."

"What actually happened? Why didn't you transform?" she asked.

"Something went wrong. I saw the Core; there was light sparkling. I began to recognise pulsing and feel the vibrations of the monochrome. Then it stopped. Everything just froze, and the light drained away leaving blackness."

Sketch's head sank downwards. She'd been trying not the think about the consequences of the collapse of the Core. Without any light, all the energies would have been extinguished.

"How did you get back?" asked Jackie.

"I have no idea. One minute I was stuck in the darkness, the next I felt a strong force, a pulling sensation and I reappeared in the library. Got stuck there til Monday morning when Trevor came in."

Though the next question was inevitable, Jackie was reluctant to voice it.

"Sketch…"

"Gone Jackie, they've gone. If there is no light, there is nothing. Computer says no."

Jackie put her arms around Sketch and pulled her in close.

"I know it's not the same, but you've got us. You've always got us."

Chapter 36

SKETCH SPENT the day liaising with Neil the lawyer and Begw about the library campaign. Keeping busy didn't take her mind off the fact that her life had changed forever, that her transformation was permanent. Nothing stopped her from thinking about Inco and the other energies from the Core. She struggled to believe she would never see them again. The descent of permanent darkness would have triggered a mass transformation of the energies into other entities outside of the computer, so she tried to find solace in the fact that they could be anywhere around her.

As night fell, Sketch got to work, engaging tiny screwdrivers to take apart the outside shell of the computer. If there were the tiniest spark of light remaining, she would find it.

Join my mailing list

Join my mailing list for a free short story, and news about the next book in the Your World series.

Sign up at www.anjcairns.com.

Acknowledgments

Many of my friends and relatives played an important part in making me write and finish Life in your world. Here's but a few:

My lovely beta readers Hayley Reed, Nick Kelly, Mark Soole and Melanie Kearney – you've been amazing, especially Hayley, my NaNoWriMo partner in crime. Jennie Rawlings at Serifim Design who created the gorgeous cover art which makes me and others smile. Steve Riley for fixing my website when the energies were messing around with the Internet. Nichola Charalambou of Creative Writes for rekindling my love of words. Charlie of Urban Writers' Retreat for space to write, and the chance to meet lovely fellow writers. Shaun Brady for your belief that I could do this, and the best hugs. And last but most certainly not least, my mum Janie, for a creating my love of all things books.

About the Author

Anj Cairns lives in North London, loves all things books, writing, reading and food.

Follow, Like, contact, love

www.anjcairns.com
anj@anjcairns.com

Printed in Great Britain
by Amazon